P Melia

The Origin Persecutions and Doctrines of the Waldenses

P Melia

The Origin Persecutions and Doctrines of the Waldenses

ISBN/EAN: 9783742802361

Manufactured in Europe, USA, Canada, Australia, Japa

Cover: Foto ©Raphael Reischuk / pixelio.de

Manufactured and distributed by brebook publishing software
(www.brebook.com)

P Melia

The Origin Persecutions and Doctrines of the Waldenses

THE ORIGIN PERSECUTIONS AND

DOCTRINES OF THE

WALDENSES.

"Nothing is covered that shall not be revealed ; nor hid that shall not be known."—*St. Matthew* x. 26.

THE ORIGIN

PERSECUTIONS AND DOCTRINES OF

THE WALDENSES

FROM DOCUMENTS,

MANY NOW THE FIRST TIME COLLECTED AND EDITED,

BY

PIUS MELIA, D.D.

LONDON:

JAMES TOOVEY, 177, PICCADILLY.

1870.

LONDON PRINTED:—PRINTED BY WHITTINGHAM AND WILKINS.
TOOKS COURT, CHANCERY LANE.

TO HIS HIGHNESS

PRINCE LOUIS LUCIEN BONAPARTE,

AS A TRIBUTE

TO HIS UNRIVALLED PHILOLOGICAL LEARNING,

THIS VOLUME IS,

WITH PERMISSION, DEDICATED

BY HIS

OBLIGED AND OBEDIENT SERVANT,

THE AUTHOR.

PREFACE.

IT was on the 30th April of last year, that in a
leading article of a London newspaper (the
"Daily Telegraph," 30th April, 1868), I read
the following expressions relating to the Waldenses of Piemont. "For sixteen hundred years, at least,
the Waldenses have guarded the pure and primitive Christianity of the Apostles. . . No one knows when or how the
faith was first delivered to these mountaineers. . . Irenæus,
Bishop of Lyons, in the second century found them a church.
. . . These gallant hill-men have kept the tradition of the
Gospel committed to them as pure and inviolate as the snow
upon their own Alps. . . . They have maintained an Evangelical form of Christianity from the very first, rejecting
image worship, invocation of saints, auricular confession,
celibacy, papal supremacy or infallibility, and the dogma of
purgatory; taking the Scripture as the rule of life, and admitting no sacraments but Baptism and the Lord's Supper . . .
No bloodier cruelty disgraces the records of the Papacy than
the persecutions endured by the ancestors of the twenty
thousand Waldenses now surviving. . . . Never did men
suffer more for their belief. . . ."

The quoted expressions not being in accordance with

my former knowledge of the Waldensian history, I imposed
upon myself the task of collecting as many books bearing
on the subject as I could find, in order to ascertain whether
my old impressions were wrong, or the greatest part of the
above assertions unfounded.

The following are the principal books I have read through
relating to this object: Jean Paul Perrin, "Histoire des
Vaudois," Geneve, 1619; Alexander Ross, "ΠΑΝΣΕΒΕΙΑ,"
London, 1653; Samuel Morland, "The History of the
Evangelical Churches of the Valleys of Piemont," London,
1658; Jean Leger, Pasteur, &c., "Histoire Generale des
Eglises Evangeliques de Piemont," Amsterdam, 1680; P.
Allix, D.D., "History of the ancient Churches of Piedmont,"
London, 1690; William Jones, "History of the Waldenses,"
London, 1812; Jean Rodolphe Peyran, Pastor, with appen-
dices by Rev. Thomas Sims, M.A., "An Historical Defence
of the Waldenses or Vaudois," London, 1826; Rev. J. L.
Jackson, M.A., "Remarks on the Vaudois of Piemont,"
London, 1826; William Stephen Gilly, M.A., "Narrative of
an Excursion to the Mountains of Piemont," London, 1827;
"Recherches Historiques sur la veritable Origine des Vaudois,
par Monseigneur Charvaz," Paris et Lyon, 1836; Robert
Baird, D.D., "Sketches of Protestantism in Italy," New
York—British edition, London, 1847; Antoine Monastier,
"A History of the Vaudois, translated from the French,"
London, 1848; Alberto Bert, Ministro, "J. Valdesi, ovvero
i Cristiani Cattolici secondo la Chiesa Primitiva," Torino,
1849; Alexis Muston, D.D., Pastor, "The Israel of the Alps,"
the Vaudois of Piemont," translated by Montgomery, A.M.,
Glasgow, 1857; E. Enderson, D.D., "The Vaudois, &c.,
Observations," London, 1858; F. M. "The Israel of the
Alps: a History of the Waldenses," London, 1863.

Beside these works, I have consulted some of the known dictionaries and encyclopedias, viz., " Le grand Dictionnaire Historique ou Melange curieux de l'Histoire, sacre et profane," par M. Louis Moreri, tom. viii. p. 47-8, à Amsterdam, 1780; "Encyclopedie methodique, par une Société de gens de lettres, de savans, d'artistes, &c., Histoire," tome cinquieme, Paris, 1791; " The Cabinet Cyclopedia," History, by the Rev. Henry Stebbing, A.M., vol. ii., London, 1834; " The Encyclopædia Metropolitana, or Universal Dictionary of Knowledge," vol. xi.; " History and Biography," vol. iii., London, 1845; " The English Cyclopedia," conducted by Charles Knight, Biography, vol. v., London, 1857 ; " Dizionario di Erudizione Ecclesiastica," del Cav⁰ Gaetano Moroni, vol. lxxxvii., Venezia, 1858, p. 212; and "The Popular Encyclopedia, or Conversation Lexicon," new and revised edition, vol. vi., London, Glasgow, and Edinburgh, 1862; and other dictionaries and biographies. I have also read on the subject many writers on Ecclesiastical history, both Catholic and Protestant.

However, before assenting to the statements of the above writers, I undertook another and much more troublesome labour; namely, that of consulting the principal authors quoted by them, and of reading their original works. And, as I could not obtain all of them in England, I went to Italy, and was fortunate enough to find them partly in the Roman libraries, but principally in the King's library of Turin; where I was allowed, by that learned and courteous librarian, Commendatore Proni, to make extracts from some authentic, but not yet published, manuscripts bearing upon the Waldensian history.

But what induced me more than anything else to publish, not all, but the most clear and undoubtedly genuine·

documents so collected, was the precious little work of
Professor James Henthorn Todd, senior Fellow of Trinity
College, Dublin, entitled " The Book of the Vaudois: the
Waldensian Manuscripts," London and Cambridge, 1865; and
the notice given there of the long lost Morland manuscripts,
lately discovered by Mr. Henry Bradshaw, M.A., Fellow of
King's College, Cambridge, and librarian of that University.

Upon my return from Italy, towards the end of last year,
I was introduced by a friend to Mr. Bradshaw, who kindly
showed me the Waldensian manuscripts, which, by the same
acute and fortunate discoverer, are truly called " the oldest
extant relics of the Vaudois literature," and I must add,
" the most important documents relating to their history."

I have thought it necessary to say all these things, to
show to the learned reader the full reliance which is to be
placed on the Documents, which I have with some labour extracted from the originals, and which I now present faithfully to the public in relation to *the Origin, the Persecutions,
and the Doctrines* of the Waldenses in the Valleys of Piemont.

If, from the evidence of the Documents, there should
follow a conclusion contrary to the assertions of writers till
now considered of authority, I beg the reader to bear in
mind, with the old Christian philosopher and martyr, Justin,
that " Reason commands those, who are truly good and
lovers of wisdom, to cultivate and love truth alone, casting
aside the opinions of their ancestors, if they are wrong;" and
that " We are not allowed to honour men more than truth."*

* *Praescribit ratio ut qui vere pii et philosophi sunt, verum unice colant et
diligant, recusantes majorum opiniones sequi, si pravae sint* (Apologia I. ad
Antoninum Pium, § VII.)

Plus honoris non est habendum homini quam veritati (Apologia II. pro Christianis, from Socrates).

I conclude by saying with another glorious martyr, Irenæus, Bishop of Lyons, " That from me, while writing in a
tongue very different from my native language, nobody
must expect graces of style which I have not acquired, or
force of expressions which I cannot pretend to, nor a choice
of words and eloquence which I do not possess; I only wish
that the Documents which, with a simple translation and
some not unnecessary remarks and comments, I publish for
love of truth, be read and accepted in the same spirit." *

P. MELIA.

14, *Gray's Inn Square*,
   November 1st, 1869.

---

* *Non autem requires a nobis qui apud Celtas commoramur . . . orationis artem quam non didicimus, neque vim conscriptionis quam non affectamus, neque ornatum verborum neque suadelam quam nescimus, sed simpliciter et vere et idiotice, quae tibi cum dilectione scripta sunt, cum dilectione percipias.* (In Præfatione, Adversus Hæreses.)

CONTENTS.

PART THE SECOND.

ON THE PERSECUTIONS OF THE WALDENSES.

Part the Third.

THE RELIGIOUS DOCTRINES OF THE WALDENSES.

THE ORIGIN OF THE WALDENSES.

SECTION I.

AUTHORITY OF RICHARD MONK OF CLUNY.

ET us begin with a document from the Chronicle of Richard, Monk of Cluny, published by Muratori ("Rerum Italicarum Scriptores," tom. iii. p. 447, *et seq.* Mediolani, 1723) from the manuscripts of the learned Bernard Guidoni, who lived from the year 1260 to the year 1331. Richard flourished about 1156, according to Martinus Polonus, Valaterranus, and Vossius: and Muratori (*Ibid.*), on the ground of his having written, not only the life of Alexander III. who died 1181, but also that of Innocent III., who died 1216, argues that Richard must have lived writing at least to the last mentioned year. That the lives of the two Popes were written, not by Guidoni, but by the monk Richard, is evident from the following statement, written in large red letters immediately after the two lives: *Huc usque Chronica Richardi Monachi Cluniacensis protenditur et terminatur.* Now, in the life of Alexander, exalted to the Pontifical Chair in 1159, there is the following clear account of the origin of the Waldenses, written, as we have said, by Richard, a respectable contemporary, and preserved for us by Guidoni, a Bishop, compared to the first Fathers of the Church for his prudence,

B

learning, and virtues: (*Assimilatus. Patribus primitivis*) (see Muratori, *ibid.* p. 274).

"About the year of Our Lord 1170[1] arose the sect and heresy of those who are called Waldenses, or Poor of Lyons. The author and founder of them was a citizen of Lyons called Waldensis,[2] from whom his followers received the like name. He being a man possessing riches, abandoning everything, resolved to live a life of poverty, and Evangelical perfection, as the Apostles did. And having caused the Gospels, and some other books of the Bible, and several authorities of Saints, which he called *Summas*, to be written for his own use in the vernacular tongue; he reading them often by himself, and little understanding them; proud in his own conceit, and possessing a little learning; assumed to himself and usurped the office of the Apostles: preaching the Gospel

---

Circa annum Domini MCLXX. *incepit secta et heresis illorum qui dicuntur Valdenses, seu Pauperes de Lugduno, cujus auctor et inventor fuit quidam civis Lugdunensis nomine Valdensis, a quo sectatores ejus fuerunt taliter nominati; qui dives rebus artifit et relictis omnibus, proponuit servare paupertatem et perfectionem Evangelicam sicut Apostoli servaverunt. Et cum fecisset sibi conscribi Evangelia et aliquos libros Bibliæ in vulgari et novarullas auctoritates Sanctorum quas summas appellavit, en aspicos eorum legens et minus eas intelligens, sensu suo inflatus cum esset medicum literatus, Apostolorum sibi officium usurpavit atque praerumpuit, per vicos et plateas Evangelia*

---

[1] As the author mentions the year 1170 as the beginning of the sect, and other authors, instead, point out 1160, and many hint other years between the two, and some others 1180, we may say that these also put the beginning of the Waldenses sect in the year 1160 speak of the first change in Peter Waldensis' life from riches to poverty, and the others, who mark the year 1170, allude to the public spreading of the sect. After which time the Waldenses were restrained or condemned many times; principally by Alexander III. in the third Council of Lateran, in 1179; by John Belesmayne or Bellismanus, Archbishop of Lyons in 1182 or 1183; by Pope Lucius III. in a Council in Verona, in 1184; by Innocent III. in the twelfth General Council, which was the fourth Lateran, in 1215; where (in the Decree III. de Hæreticis) the Waldenses are described as persons having the appearance, without the reality, of

godliness; and by Pope Gregory IX. in 1234. in a Commission (Decret. L. v. Tit. vii. de Hæret.), with these words: *Excommunicamus et anathematizamus universos hæreticos, Catharos, Patarinos, Pauperes de Lugduno, &c. Damnamus vero per Ecclesiam Seculari judicio relinquentur, animadversione debita puniendi.*

[2] Peter Waldensis, or Waldensis, or de Vaulx, or Valdo, or Vaudois (different manner of spelling the same name by different writers), was a citizen of Lyons in fact, though born in a little village near Lyons, on the Rhone. He had his dwelling-house in Lyons near the church of St. Nizier, in a street, which, after his expulsion, was called *Rue Maudite*, till the fourteenth century, when it was named *Rue Vendrant.* (See Guy Allard, "Bibl. du Dauphiné," Charles, vol. ii. p. 69, Paradin, p. 121; and Perrins's documents, in the Liber. of Lyons.)

in the streets and in the squares. He caused many men and women to become his accomplices in a like presumption: whom he sent to preach as his disciples. They being simple and illiterate people, traversing the villages and entering into the houses, spread everywhere many errors. Called to account by the Archbishop of Lyons, John Beles-Mayus, they were prohibited by him. But they would not obey, offering as a pretext for their folly, that they ought to obey not men but God, who commanded the Apostles to preach the Gospel to every creature: arrogating to themselves what had been said to the Apostles, of whom, by a feigned appearance of poverty and sanctity, they professed to be followers and successors, despising the Clergy and Priests. Thus, from the presumptuous usurpation of the office of preaching, they became first disobedient, afterwards contumacious, and therefore being excommunicated, were exiled from that country. At last, cited to a Council which was held in Rome before that of Lateran, they were adjudged contumacious and schismatics. And being dispersed through the provinces, and mingling on the borders of Lombardy with other heretics, and also imbibing and following their errors, were adjudged heretics.

---

prædicando; multosque homines et mulieres ad similem præsumptionem complices sibi fecit, quos ad prædicandum tanquam discipulos omittebat. Qui cum essent idiotæ et illiterati, per villas discurrentes et domos penetrantes, multos errores circumquaque diffuderunt; et vocati ab Archiepiscopo Lugdunensi Domino Johanne Beles-Mayus, prohibiti sunt ab eodem; sed obedire minime voluerunt, velamen suæ cæcitatis prætendentes et dicentes quod oporteret magis Deo quam hominibus obedire, qui præcepit Apostolis, omni creaturæ Evangelium prædicare; arrogantes sibi quod Apostolis erat dictum; quorum imitatores et successores, falsa paupertatis professione et ficta sanctitatis imagine, se esse profitebantur; aspernantes Clericos et Presbyteros. Sic itaque ex præsumptuosa usurpatione officii prædicandi, inobedientes, deinde contumaces et exinde excommunicati, ab illa patria sunt expulsi. Demum vero convocati ad Concilium quod fuit Romæ ante Lateranense celebratum, fuerunt pertinaces et schismatici judicati. Simque dispersi per provincias, et in confinibus Lombardiæ cum aliis hereticis se miscentes et eorum errores bibentes et sectantes, fuerunt hæretici judicati."

HE second document relating to the Origin of the Waldenses is given by Father Moneta, whose manuscripts, in the libraries of the Vatican, of Bologna, and of Naples, have been published by Thomas Augustin Ricchini in Rome, 1743, under the title, " *Venerabilis Patris Moneta Cremonensis Ordinis Prædicatorum adversus Catharos et Waldenses, Libri quinque.*" Father Moneta was a professor of philosophy in Bologna in 1218, when, at the preaching of the blessed Reginaldus Aurelianensis, he was induced to abandon his secular pursuits, and two years afterwards gave his name to the Dominican Order. St. Dominic appointed him to be his vicar in Milan, and through Insubria; and it is said that the holy founder died in Bologna in the very bed of F. Moneta. F. Moneta's learning, zeal and virtues, and chiefly his patience when he became blind, are praised by many writers of his time. The year in which he wrote his work is clearly stated by him, when (Lib. III. cap. iii. § ii.), after quoting the saying of our Lord: "I saw Satan falling from heaven like a flash of lightning," the author continues: "But He (our Lord) did not see the fall of Sathan with his human eyes, because it is not more than twelve hundred and forty-four years that he was incarnate." (In the Vat. MS.), *Sed non videbat eum cadentem secundum homo, non enim sunt plusquam 1244 anni quod Ipse factus est homo:* from which F. Moneta derives a proof of the eternal divinity of our Lord. Now this epoch of 1244 is to be marked, both because it gives us the date in which F. Moneta wrote his book, and it helps us to understand an important part of the following passage (Lib. v. cap. i. § iv. pp. 402, 403):

"Having proved that the community of the Catharites is not the Church of God, let us prove that the community of

the Poor Lyonists is not the Church of God. This appears
from what is said in the second letter of St. Peter the
Apostle (chapter ii. 1 and 10): 'Who shall bring in sects
of perdition, and despise authority.' Secondly, the same
thing is proved if their Origin is attended to; because it is
clear that they had their beginning from Waldesius, a
citizen of Lyons, who entered on this path not more than
eighty years ago; or, if they are more or less, the difference
of more or less is little.' Consequently, they are not the
successors of the primitive Church, and of course they are
not the Church of God. And if they should say that their
manner of proceeding was before Waldesius, let them prove it
with some testimony, which they cannot do. Thirdly, it may
be demonstrated that their congregation is not the Church of
God through the remission of sins. . . . You come from
Waldesius, tell us, from whence did he come?' . . . If they
say that they came forth from God and from the Apostles
and from the Gospel, the fact is against them, because God forgives sins through his minister (John xx. 23): 'To whom you
shall forgive their sins, are forgiven to them.' Therefore, if
God forgave the sins of Waldesius, He forgave them through

" Ostendo quod universitas Catharorum non est Ecclesia Dei, ostendamus
quod universitas Pauperum Lewisianum non est Ecclesia Dei. Et probatur
per illud (2 Petri ii. 1, 10): Qui introducent sectas perditionis . . . domi-
nationemque contemnunt. . . . Secundo modo id ostenditur si ipsorum origo
attendatur. Non enim multum temporis est quod esse ceperunt. Quoniam
sicut patet a Valderio cive Lugdunensi exordium acceperunt, qui hanc viam
inceepit non esse plures quam octoginta anni; vel si plures aut pauciores,
parum plures vel pauciores existunt. Ergo non sunt successores Ecclesiæ
primitiæ, ergo non sunt Ecclesia Dei. Si autem dicant quod sua vita ante
Valdenium fuit, ostendant hoc aliquo testimonio, quod minime facere possunt.
. . . Tertio per remissionem peccatorum ostendi potest quod eorum congregatio
non est Ecclesia Dei . . . Vos venistis a Valderio; dicatis unde ipse venit?
. . . Si dicant quod a Deo venerunt et ab Apostolis atque Evangelio, contra:

' Taking 80 from 1244 we have the year
1164, more or less. Now this perfectly
agrees with the document first quoted, in
which the Origin of the Waldenses is put
about the year of our Lord 1170.

' Here the author repeats the fable forged

by the Waldenses, that one of their chiefs,
Peter, went to the Pope, and promised to
him that they would hold to the four Doctors
Ambrose, Augustin, Gregory, and Jerome;
and that the Pope gave him the office of
preaching.

His minister. But tell me through whom of His ministers did God forgive him his sins? Fourthly, the same is proved from the Ecclesiastical Orders, of which they confess that there are three at least—Episcopacy, Priesthood, and Deaconship. Without these three Orders the Church of God cannot and ought not to exist, as they admit. Let us, then, say to them: If the Church of God is not without these Orders, and you are without them, it follows that your congregation is not the Church of God. If they should say that their congregation has Orders, I ask, From whom did they receive them? Who, then, is your Bishop? If they should name a particular man, I ask again, Who gave him the Ordination? If they name some other, I equally ask, Who ordained this other? And, so going on, they will be obliged to ascend to Waldesius. Next, it is to be asked, From whence had he his Orders? If they answer that he had them by himself, it is clear that it is against the Apostle, who says (Heb. v. 4): ' And no one assumes the honour, except him who is called by the Lord, like Aaron.' . . . If, then, Waldesius had the Orders from himself, he glorified himself to be a Bishop; in consequence, he was an antichrist, namely, against Christ and his Church. And if they should say that Waldesius had his Orders from God directly, their assertion cannot be confirmed by any testi-

---

Ipse non parcit nisi per ministrum ; unde : ' Quorum remiseritis peccata remittentur eis' (John. xx. 23). Ergo si remisit Valdesio, per ministrum remisit. Sed dic mihi, per quem ministrum si remisit? Quarto modo idem ostenditur per Ordinem Ecclesiasticum, quem ipsi ad minus triplicem confitentur, scilicet Episcopatum, Presbyteratum et Diaconatum, sine quo triplici ordine Ecclesia Dei non potest esse nec debet, ut ipsi testantur. Dicemus ergo eis: Si Ecclesia Dei non est sine istis ordinibus, vestra autem generatio sine eis est, ergo non est Ecclesia Dni. Si autem dicant : Nostra generatio illos habet, quaero a quo habuit? Quis enim est episcopus vester? Si dicant, talis homo; dicite quis ordinavit eum? Si dicunt: Quidam; quaero etiam, Quis istum alium ordinavit? Et sic ascendendo compelluntur usque ad Valdesium venire. Postea quaerendum est, Unde iste ordines habuit? Si dicunt quod a seipso, palam est, si hoc est; quia contrarius Apostolo sit, qui dicit (Heb. v. 4). Nec quisquam sumit sibi honorem, sed qui vocatur a Deo tamquam Aaron. . . . Valdesius autem si a se Ordinem habuit, clarificavit semetipsum et pontifex fieret. Ipse igitur antichristus fuit, idest Christo et Ecclesiae ejus

mony of Scripture. . . . Some said that Waldesius received
his Orders from the community of his brethren. The first
who said so was one chief of the poor Lombards, called
Thomas, a perverted doctor, and he endeavoured to prove
it thus : Every member of his congregation could give
Waldesius the right of a ruler over himself, and so all the
congregation could give, and really gave to Waldesius, the
rights of a ruler over them all; and thus he was made their
pontiff and prelate. But if that heresiarch had understood
how foolish that reason was, he would not have allowed
himself to utter those words; because every Bishop has the
right of being a ruler, but not every ruler has the right of
being a Bishop. From the assertion that they could give
him the office of a ruler, it does not follow that they could
make him a Bishop. . . . One thing is to confer Orders
and another to give domination. Orders are given by a
Bishop only. . . . It appears, then, that it is a falsehood
to say that Waldesius received Orders, and that he could
give them to others. He had no Orders, and, consequently,
you have no Orders, and you cannot be the Church of God,
in which there are three Orders at least. Perhaps (*ibid.*
§ v. p. 407) they might say that their congregation and
the congregation of the Church of Rome are *one, holy* and

---

contrarius. Si dicunt quoniam a Deo Ordinem habuit immediate; illud
nullo testimonio Scripturæ ostendere possunt. Sciendum autem quod quidam
dixerunt quod Valdesius ordinem habuit ob universitate fratrum suorum.
Horum autem qui hoc dixerunt auctor fuit quidam heresiarcha Pauperum
Lombardorum, doctor perversus Thomas nomine. Hoc autem probare taliter
nisus est : Quilibet de illa congregatione potuit dare Valdesio jus suum, scilicet
regere seipsum; et sic tota congregatio illa potuit conferre et contulit Valdesio
regimen omnium, et sic creaverunt illum omnium pontificem et prælatum. Si
autem heresiarcha ille intellexisset quam fatuum istud esset, nequaquam ab
ore suo istud procedere permisisset. Omnis enim pontificatus est regimen,
sed non omne regimen est pontificatus. Quomodo ergo sequitur; potuerunt
ei dare regimen sui, ergo pontificatum. . . . Aliud est conferre Ordinem, et
aliud conferre regimen; primum enim tantum Episcoporum est . . . Unde
palam est quia fabulosum est dicere quod Valdesius Ordinem habuit, et quod
aliis conferre potuerit. Sic ergo ordine caruit : ergo et vos, ergo non estis
Ecclesia Dei, quæ in tribus Ordinibus ad minus consistit, (Ibid. § v. p. 407.)
Forte dicerent quod eorum congregatio et congregatio Romanæ Ecclesiæ est

Catholic, though they are divided into two parts : one part malignant, which now is called the Roman Church ; one part benignant, which is the Waldensian congregation. But against this assertion there is the fact that the latter (namely, the Waldensian congregation) had no existence from the time of Silvester to the time of Waldesius, which you cannot disprove. Therefore the Church failed with Silvester, and it is shown to be false in the third chapter. . . . These heretics (chap. iii. § i. p. 412) say that the Church of God failed at the time of blessed Silvester . . . and that it has been restored in these times by themselves, the first of whom Waldesius was. Let us then ask from whence they know that the Church failed. And, as they have no testimony to confirm it, they will be reduced to silence. Let us show (*ibid.* § ii. p. 413) that the Church of the New Testament, from the time of her beginning, did not fail to exist : 'The Lord God (Luke i. 32, 33) shall give Him (to Jesus Christ) the seat of David His father, . . . and of His kingdom there shall be no end.' And Daniel (chap. ii. 44) : 'In the days of those kingdoms God will raise the kingdom of heaven, which shall never be destroyed, and His kingdom shall not be delivered up to another people, . . . and itself shall stand for ever.' (*Ibid.* § iii.) 'A bad life does not take away the power attached to the ministry.' Hence,

---

una, sancta et catholica, licet duæ sint ejus partes : una est pars maligna quæ dicitur modo Romana Ecclesia, alia benigna quæ est congregatio Valdensium. Sed contra. Illa pars a tempore Silvestri non fuit usque ad tempus Valdesii, quod in posuis ostendere ; Ergo Ecclesia defecit in Silvestro ; quod falsum esse ostenditur in tertio capite. (Ibid. Lib. v. Cap. iii. § i. p. 412.) Isti hæretici dicunt, Ecclesiam Dei, tempore beati Silvestri defecisse . . . . in temporibus autem istis restitutam esse per ipsos, quorum primus fuit Valdesius, Quæramus ergo, unde habeat quod defecerit ? Et cum inde testimonium non habeant, obmutescent. Ostendamus (Ibid. § ii. p. 413) quod Ecclesia Novi Testamenti postquam esse cœpit, non desierit esse : ' Dabit illi Dominus Deus sedem David patris ejus . . . et regni ejus non erit finis (Luc. i. 32, 83.). In diebus autem regnorum illorum suscitabit Deus cœli regnum, quod in æternum non dissipabitur, et regnum ejus alteri populo non tradetur . . . et ipsum stabit in æternum' (Dan. ii. 44). (Ibid § iii.) Mala vita non tollit effectum suum ministerio. Ergo, posito quod Silvester peccaverit (which

though we should admit that Silvester sinned and became
wicked (which is false), yet the Church did not fail with
Silvester.   The minister does not lose his Orders for his
sin.   'Many (Matt. vii. 22) will say to me in that day:
Lord, Lord, have not we prophesied in Thy name, and cast
out devils in Thy name, and done many miracles in Thy
name?'   They did so, not in virtue of their lives, but in
virtue of their ministry."

Section III.

F. STEVAN BORBONE DE BELLAVILLA'S TESTIMONY.

WE take the third document from the writings of
F. Stevan de Borbone, called also De Bellavilla,
from the name of a castle in Burgundy, where he
was born, towards the end of the twelfth century.   After
finishing his studies in Paris he entered into the Order of
St. Dominic, and about 1228 he was already preaching in
Lyons, and in many other places; and also on the Alps.
Famous for his virtuous life, his zeal and learning, he,
during the fourth of a century, discharged the office of a
defender of the faith in Clairmont and in Lyons.   He wrote
a great volume on the Gifts of the Holy Ghost, and ended
his life in Lyons in the year 1261.   (*See* Quetif and Echard,
"Scriptores Ordinum Praedicatorum," vol. i. Lutetiae
Parisiorum, 1719, sæc. xiii, p. 184 *et seq.*)   Before giving
Bellavilla's document on the Origin of the Waldenses, it
will not be useless to state a few particulars related by him
in the above-mentioned work bearing on our argument.   He
says that he heard (Sorb. MS. fol. 391) from a man, who

---

is denied by the author afterwards), *et malus factus fuerit, non tamen defecit
Ecclesia in Silvestro.   Ergo non amittitur (ordo) per peccatum.   'Multi
dicent mihi in illa die: Domine, Domine: nonne in nomine tuo prophetavimus,
et in nomine tuo dæmonia ejecimus et in nomine tuo virtutes multas facimus
(Matth. vii. 22.)P   Non per vitam sed per ministerium.*"

assured him that he was present on the occasion, that in a town of Lombardy there were seven chiefs of different sects, opposed to each other, who, at a meeting held by them, tried each one to establish his own doctrine, and to show the falsehood of the others; and that everyone concluded his speech by excommunicating everybody else, if they should propose or accept anything contrary to his belief. He also relates that in the town called Joinville (*super Saponam in Diæcesi Bisuntinensi (Bisanzon)* appeared a man in disguise, who, being summoned before a magistrate and obliged to give an account of himself, admitted that for eighteen years he had been absent from the place in order to study in Milan the tenets of the Waldensian sect; that there were seventeen sects, everyone contrary to the others, which sects were also condemned by those of his sect (and he gave the names of them all); and that he was of the sect of those called the *Poor of Lyons*, who also call themselves *Poor of Spirit*, who, from the name of their chief, are called *Waldenses*, who, amongst other errors, condemn every person possessing earthly goods. *Prima, de qua ipse erat, dicebantur Pauperes de Lugduno, qui se etiam vocant Pauperes Spiritu, qui dicuntur Valdenses a suo hæresiarcha, qui cum aliis erroribus suis damnant omnes terrena possidentes* (L. C.). But let us hear on the subject F. Steven Borbone de Bellavilla in the thirty-first chapter of his work already quoted.

" Fourthly, we ought to speak of the heretics of our time, namely of the Waldenses, whence they had their beginning, and from whom and why and how they are so called. From the author of this heresy named Waldensis, they are called Waldenses. They are also called Poor of Lyons, because they began to profess poverty there. They call themselves

---

"Quarto dicendum est de hæreticis nostri temporis scilicet *Waldensibus* . . . unde ortum habuerunt, et unde et quare et quomodo appellentur. *Waldenses autem* dicti sunt a primo hujus hæresis auctore qui nominatus fuit *Waldensis*. Dicuntur etiam Pauperes de Lugduno, quia ibi inceperunt in professione paupertatis. Vocant autem se " Pauperes Spiritu," propter quod Dominus

Poor of Spirit, because our Lord said (Matt. v.) 'Blessed are the poor of spirit.' Truly poor in their spirit, without any spiritual good and without the Holy Ghost. That sect took its origin in the following way, as I have been told by many who knew their elders, and by that Priest who was much respected and rich in the town of Lyons, and was a friend of our brethren, Bernard Ydros by name, who, when he was young and a transcriber,[*] wrote for money for the said Waldensis the first books possessed by the Waldenses in the old Provençal language. The translator, under whose dictation the books were written, was Steven de Ansa (or de Emsa, MS. Rotom.), whom I have often seen. He afterwards obtained an Ecclesiastical benefice in the Cathedral of Lyons, and falling from the roof of a house, which he was building, he was suddenly killed. A rich man in the said town, called Waldensis, hearing the Gospels, and having a little learning, desirous to know their contents, made a bargain with these Priests, that the one should translate the Gospels into the vernacular language, and the other should write under the dictation of the first. They did so; and with the Gospels they also translated many other books of the Bible, and many authorities of Saints united under titles which they

---

dicit (Matt. v.) ' *Beati pauperes spiritu.' Et vere pauperes in spiritu a spiritualibus bonis et a Spiritu Sancto. Incepit autem illa secta per hunc modum, secundum quod ego a pluribus qui priores eorum viderunt, et a Sacerdote illo qui satis honoratus erat et dives in civitate Lugdunensi, et amicus fratrum nostrorum, qui dictus fuit Bernardus Ydros : qui, cum esset juvenis et scriptor, scripsit dicto Waldensi priores libros pro pecunia in Romano quos ipsi habuerunt, transferente et dictante ei Stephano de Ansa (Cod. Rotomag. de Emsa), qui postea beneficiatus in Ecclesia majore Lugdunensi (Cod. Rotom. promotus est in Sacerdotem ei), de solario domus quam ædificabat corruens, morte subita ritam finivit, quem ego vidi sæpe. Quidam dives rebus in dicta urbe dictus Waldensis audiens Evangelia, cum non esset multum litteratus, curiosus intelligere quid dicerent, fecit pactum cum dictis sacerdotibus, alteri ut transferret ei in vulgari, alteri ut scriberet quæ ille dictaret : quod fecerunt. Similiter multos libros Biblicos, et auctoritates Sanctorum multas per titulos congregatas, quas Sententias appellabant.*

---

[*] In that age, in which the art of printing was unknown, it was a respected and useful profession to be a good transcriber.

called *Sentences.* Now the same citizen, often reading those writings and learning them by heart, resolved to keep Evangelical perfection as the Apostles did. He sold every thing he had, and through contempt of this world threw his money into the streets to the poor: and preaching the Gospels and what he had learned by heart, presumptuously assumed the office of the Apostles. So he succeeded in gathering together men and women: and teaching them the Gospels, induced them to do the same: and though they were of a very low state and profession, he sent them to preach through the surrounding villages. They, men and women, silly and illiterate, going here and there through the country, entering into the houses, and preaching in the squares and also in the Churches, induced others to do the same. But as by their temerity and ignorance, they spread many errors and scandals all around, they were called to account by the Bishop of Lyons, named John, who commanded them not to dare to explain the Scriptures nor to preach any more. They defended themselves with the answer of the Apostles (Act. v.); and their master assuming to himself the ministry of St. Peter, answered, as St. Peter did to the chief Priests: *It is necessary to obey God rather than men: God commanded the Apostles to preach the Gospel to every creature.* As if our

Quæ cum dictus civis sæpe legeret et corde tenus firmaret, proposuit servare perfectionem Evangelicam, ut Apostoli servaverunt. Qui rebus suis omnibus venditis, in contemptum mundi, per lutum pauperibus promiam suam projiciebat; et officium Apostolorum usurpavit et præsumpsit; Evangelio et ea quæ corde retinueral per vicos et plateas prædicando, multos homines et mulieres ad idem faciendum ad se convertendo, firmans eis Evangelia. Quos etiam per villas circumjacentes mittebat ad prædicandum vilissimorum quorumcumque officiorum. Qui etiam tam homines quam mulieres idiotæ et illiterati per villas discurrentes et domos penetrantes et in plateis prædicantes et etiam in Ecclesiis, ad idem alios provocabant. Cum autem eo temeritate sua et ignorantia multos errores et scandala circumquaque diffunderent venati ab episcopo Lugdunensi, qui Joannes vocabatur, prohibuit eis ne intromitterent se de Scripturis exponendis vel prædicandis. Ipsi autem recurrentes et responsionem Apostolorum (Act. v.) et magister eorum usurpans Petri officium; sicut ipse respondit principibus sacerdotum; ait; Obedire oportet magis Deo quam hominibus qui præceperat Apostolis, prædicare Evangelium omni creaturæ (Marci in fine). Quasi hoc diceret Dominus eis quod diceret

Lord had said to them what he said to the Apostles; who
notwithstanding did not dare to preach till they received
virtue from on High, till they were gifted with perfect wisdom, and had the gift of speaking every language. They
then, namely Waldensis and his followers, through presumption and the assumption of the office of the Apostles,
became at first disobedient, afterwards obstinate, and finally
were excommunicated. Exiled from that place they were
then cited to appear at the Council, which was held in Rome
before the Lateran. As they were obstinate, they were adjudged schismatic. Afterwards mixing with other heretics,
and imbibing and spreading their errors in the land of Provence and in Lombardy, they were pronounced heretics.
They are hostile and noxious to the Church in the highest
degree, they spread everywhere, appearing to have holiness
and faith without professing its truth; so much more dangerous because they are concealed, because they cunningly
disguise themselves in different ways and disguises. It
happened sometimes that one of their chiefs was imprisoned,
who had in his possession many means of fictious disguises,
with which he assumed different forms like Protheus. If
he was persecuted as wearing a particular form of dress, and
it was reported to him, he appeared transformed. Now he
had a dress and the usual attire of a pilgrim, now he had

---

*Apostolis ; qui tamen prædicare non præsumpserunt, usquequo induti virtute
ex alto fuerunt, usquequo perfectissimo et plenissimo scientiâ perlustrati
fuerunt, et donum linguarum omnium susceperunt. Ii ergo, Waldensis
scilicet et sui, primo ex præsumptione et officii Apostolici usurpatione, exti-
terunt in inobedientiam, demum in contumaciam, demum in excommunicationis sententiam. Post expulsi ab illa terra, ad concilium quod fuit Romæ
ante Lateranum vocati et pertinaces, fuerunt schismatici postea judicati.
Postea in Provinciæ terra et Lombardiæ cum aliis hæreticis se admiscentes,
et errorem eorum bibentes et serentes hæretici sunt judicati. Ecclesiæ infes-
tissimi et periculosissimi, ubique discurrentes, speciem sanctitatis et fidei prætendentes, veritatem autem ejus non habentes ; tanto periculosiores quanto
occultiores, se sub diversis hominum habitibus et artificiis transfigurantes.
Aliquando quidem maximus inter eos fuit captus qui secum ferebat multorum
artificiorum indicia, in quo quasi Proteus se transfigurabat. Si quæreretur
in una similitudine et ei innotesceret, in aliam se transmutabat. Aliquando*

the stick and the iron of a penitent man; now he had the
fictitious habit of a shoemaker, now of a barber, now of a
mower, &c. The others are doing the same. This sect
began in the year of our Lord 1170, or (as it is in MS. Rotom.)
1180⁴ under John Bolesmanis or Belesmanis, Archbishop of
Lyons."

SECTION IV.

ABBOT BERNARD'S EVIDENCE.

URTHER evidence relating to the time in which
the Waldenses made their first appearance, is
given to us by an old Abbot who had his title
from the Abbey called Chaud Fountain (Fontis Calidi). His
manuscripts were published by Jacob Gretzer, S. J. and are
printed in the Great Library of the Fathers (" Bibliotheca
Veterum Patrum," &c. vol. xxv. p. 1585, *et seq.* Lugduni,
1677). It is supposed that he wrote his book towards
the end of the twelfth century. His work bears this title,
" Bernardus Abbas Fontis Calidi adversus Valdensium sectam." In twelve chapters he relates and confutes the errors
for which the Waldenses were condemned by Bernard Archbishop of Narbonne after a discussion which took place under
the presidency of Raymundus de Deventria a Priest of high

---

*ferebat habitum et signacula peregrini, aliquando baculum prenitentiarii et
ferramenta, aliquando se fingebat sutorem, aliquando barbitonsorem, aliquando
messorem ac alii similiter idem faciunt."* *"Incepit autem haec secta ab
incarnatione Domini* MCLXX *sub Joanne dicto Bolesmanis Archiepiscopo
Lugdunensi (in Cod. Rotom.* MCLXXX *sub Joanne dicto Belesmanis), &c.*

⁴ John Belesmanis, or the Belilismanibus,
being Bishop of Poitiers in the year 1181,
was elected Archbishop of Narbonne. However, when he went to Rome to obtain the
sanction of the Pope, the clergy of Lyons
chose him to be their Archbishop and Primate.
Pope Lucius III., newly raised to the Popedom, confirmed this second election in the
year 1182, and made him Legate of the
Apostolical Chair in the kingdom of France.

John, in 1193, renounced spontaneously his
seat, and retired to the monastery of Clair
Valle, *Ubi usque ad mortem cum maxima
pietate et devotion perseveravit.* (See
"Gallia Christiana," vol. iv. p. 130, et seq.
Paris, 1728). From this notice it appears
that Belesmanis could not pronounce, in
Lyons, his sentence against the Waldenses
before the year 1182 or 1183.

respectability. He, after having heard the allegations of the two parties, gave his final sentence in writing and pronounced the Waldenses to be heretics, under the heads of which they were accused. *Auditis igitur partium allegationibus, præfatus judex per scriptum definitivam dedit sententiam, et hæreticos esse, in capitulis de quibus accusati fuerant, pronunciavit* (ibid.). In reading his statement it will be observed that he, having called the Waldenses by the name by which they were called by all contemporaries who wrote in Latin, he assumes the liberty of deriving its signification from a dense valley *a valle densa,* in order to have an opportunity of making a moral allusion to their errors. The same observation is applicable to Ebrardus Flandrensis of Betunia (another author of the same century) who in the xxvth chapter of his book, entitled " Antihæreseos," says that they called themselves *Vallenses eo quod in valle lacrymarum maneant* (see Bibl. PP. L. C. p. 1525). And as we have here related the mystical etymology given to the name *Waldensis* by these writers, let us bear in mind what is stated by the best historians about the surname of Peter the wealthy merchant of Lyons (see " Helyot, Histoire Complete des Ordres Monastiques," vol. ii. p. 283, *et seq.* Guingamp. 1839). He was a native of a village called Vaud or Vaux in Dauphiny, on the river Rhône near Lyons. Thence in his language he was called Peter de Vaud or Vaudois, and his followers are equally called Vaudois in the vernacular language from the name of their founder; and from thence most of the Latin writers gave to Peter the name of Valdensis from the Latin name of his native place, *Valdum,* and to his partisans that of *Valdenses,* changing the original " *u* " of Vaud into " *l* " and giving to the word the Latin termination " *ensis.*" It is not surprising then that the two above-mentioned writers, dividing the name Valdensis into two parts *Val* and *densis,* and adding two letters to the first part, and changing *is* into *a* at the end of the second, in order to moralize on the supposed etymology of the name, took the liberty of deriving it from *Valle densa*. Yet it must be confessed that this derivation is only a fantastical one. Let us see now and mark well the expressions of the Abbot on our subject. They are short and conclusive.

"Pope Lucius,' of happy memory, was the president of the Holy Roman Church, when new heretics suddenly raised their heads. As if it were a presage of future events, they were called Waldenses, namely, from a dense valley, because they are enveloped in the deep and dense darkness of errors. Though condemned by the said Pontiff,' with their rash daring, they spread throughout the earth the poison of their perfidiousness."

Section V.

REINERIUS SACCO'S STATEMENT.

THE fifth document is from Reinerius Sacco, of whom Quetif and Echard, in their able work on the Dominican writers ("Scriptores Ordinis Prædicatorum." Lutetiæ Parisior. 1719), say, according to Leander (fol. 148) and Antony Senensis (in Bibl. Dom.), that he was born in that part of upper Italy called Gallia Togata, in the town of Piacenza; that he was at first, for seventeen years, a chief and bishop of heretics, and caused

---

" *Sancta Romana Ecclesia providente Domino Lucio inclitæ recordationis, subito extulerunt caput novi hæretici, qui quodam præsagio futurorum dicti sunt Valdenses, viniruan a valle densa, eo quod profundis et densis errorum tenebris involvantur. Hi quamvis a profato Pontifice condemnati, rirus sua perfidia longe lateque per orbem temerario ausu eromunerunt*" (Id ib. in Præf.).

‡ Pope Lucius III. sat on the Pontifical Chair from 30 August, 1181, to 23 November, 1185.

The Waldenses were condemned, in fact, by Pope Lucius III., at a Council held in Verona, in the presence of many Bishops and of the Emperor Frederick, in the year 1184, with these words: "By Apostolical Authority, and by means of this Constitution, we do condemn every heresy, whatever name it bears, and principally the Catharists and the Patherines, and those who, with a wrong name, call themselves, with deception, the Humbled or the Poor of Lyons." *Omnem hæresim quotcunque nominibus censentur per hujus Constitutionis seriem Auctoritate Apostolica condemnamus. In primis ergo Catharos et Patherinos, et eos qui se Humiliatos vel Pauperes de Lugduno falso nomine mentiuntur.* (Sacr. Concil. Nova, et A. Catharthe, tom. xxii. Verutile, 1778.)

a great many evils to the Catholic faith in the province of
Emilia; but that, after his conversion, having entered the
Dominican Order, he defended, during the remainder of his
life, the revealed doctrine against the false principles of the
heretics with all his might, and wrote a book to the same
purpose. According to the same Dominican writers, besides
the manuscript published by Jacob Gretzer ("Ingolstadii,"
1614, in 4to.), and reprinted in the "Library of the Fathers"
("Bibliotheca Patrum," tom. xxv. p. 262 *et seq.* Lugduni,
1677), there are two other manuscripts of the same work
of Reinerius. One of them existed in their Convent at
Rouen, and was afterwards brought to Paris; the other
in the library of Trinity College, Dublin (t. ii. p. ii. 273,
133), both on parchment.[1] These last two manuscripts are
nearly identical; but Gretzer's differs from them both in
the order of the chapters and in the disposition and expressions of some sentences, though it is admitted that this
also is a genuine work of the same author, excepting the
German words interpolated here and there in the text by the
German publisher; and, we may add, excepting the mistakes
generally unavoidable when the manuscripts are very badly
written and incorrect, as Gretzer confesses is the case with
his text. Hear him in his preface (L. C.): "*Reinerii Com-
mentarium ex papyraceo quodam codice admodum vitiose exarato
exscribendum curavimus. . . . Utinam codex emendatior et
emaculatior obtigisset!*" And, in fact, the title of the book
in Gretzer's publication, "Reinerii Ordinis Prædicatorum
contra Valdenses Hæreticos Liber," does not comprehend
the argument of the author, as the greater part of the work

---

[1] The title of the work there is: Summa
Fr. Reinerii de Ordine Fratrum Prædicatorum, De Catharis et Leonistis, sive Pauperibus de Lugduno. The preface is: In
nomine D. N. J. C., cum multæ hæreti-
corum olim fuerint multæ quæ omnino fere
destructæ sunt per gratiam J. C. tamen
duæ principales modo seminantur, quarum
altera vocatur Cathari sive Patrini, et altera
Leonistæ sive Pauperes de Lugduno, quarum
opinionum præservi pagina enodantur. In
the same two manuscripts in the fifth chapter,
De Falsa Persityasio Catharorum, the author states what he was: Ego autem F.
Reinerius olim hæresiarcha, sive Dei gratia
Sacerdos licet indignus, etc., dico indubi-
tanter, quod in annis XVII. quibus conver-
satus sum cum eis, etc.

is against the Catharites. So it is with the title of the fourth chapter, "De Sectis Antiquorum Hæreticorum," which does not agree with all the names subjoined there, as there is a mixture of old and new heresies. The same Gretzer, in a long catalogue of various readings (Bibl Patr., *ibid.* p. 264), makes this addition to chapter iv.: "*Præter sectas Manichæorum et Patherinorum quæ occupant Lombardiam, et præter sectas Ortlibariorum, Runcariorum,*" &c.; and, line 61 of the said page, chapter v., at the words "*Eorum et rancor,*" is said instead, "*Eorum et Runcarii.*" So, again, in chapter vi. (*ibid.* p. 269), amongst the Catharites a certain Joannes de *Lugduno* is named; yet, in the two other MSS. above-mentioned, this John is more than once called de *Lugio* : "*De propriis opinionibus Joannis de Lugio; dictus Joannes de Lugio hæresiarcha,*" &c. I mention this in order to show the learned reader that, since the Gretzerian text is so corrupt, although under the title "De Sectis Antiquorum Hæreti-corum" there may be found some mention of the Poor of Lyons, that is no proof of their being of a greater antiquity than appears from the evidence of all other documents; and also from the following Chapter V. of the same text of Gretzer. Perhaps the adjective *antiquorum* is also a mistake.

Before reading the document, observe that in the fourth chapter of Gretzer's MS. there are the following expressions : "Amongst all these sects which now are, or have been, there is none more dangerous to the Church than that of the Leonista, and this for three reasons. First, because it has lasted longer; some people say that it has endured from the time of Silvester, and some say from the time of the Apostles." "*Inter omnes has sectas quæ adhuc sunt vel fuerunt, non est perniciosior Ecclesiæ quam Leonistarum, et hoc tribus de causis. Prima est quia diuturnior; aliqui enim dicunt quod duraverit a tempore Silvestri; aliqui a tempore Apostolorum.*" I am fully persuaded that nobody will agree with those writers,[20] who, on the strength of the passages quoted, endeavour to establish the pretended antiquity of the Waldenses. First, because the author simply relates here what some people say, *aliqui dicunt*, without giving any approval to that assertion. Secondly, because in the next chapter, in which Reinerius speaks for himself, he gives a downright denial to that opinion, as we shall presently see. The time at which the document was written is given at the end of the manuscripts mentioned by Echard (L. C.): " The above work was faithfully completed by the said brother Reinerius, the year of our Lord twelve hundred and fifty." " A.D. MCCL. *compilatum est fideliter per dictum Reinerium opus superius annotatum.*"

" Chapter V. ' Of the Sects of Modern Heretics' (Bibl. Patr. L. C., p. 264). Observe that the sect of the Poor of Lyons, who also are called Leonista, had its origin after this manner: The principal citizens in Lyons being assembled, it happened that one of their number died suddenly" in their presence. By this event one of them was so much frightened that he immediately gave a great amount of money to the poor; in consequence of which a great multitude of poor gathered around him, and he taught them to observe voluntary poverty, and to be followers of Christ and of the Apostles. And, as he was to some extent learned, he made them acquainted with the New Testament

---

Cap. V.—De sectis modernorum hereticorum. Nota quod secta Pauperum de Lugduno, qui dicti Leonistæ dicuntur, tali modo orta est. Cum circa majores pariter essent in Lugduno, contigit quidem ex eis mori subito coram eis. Unde quidam inter eos statim fuit territus quod statim magnam thesaurum pauperibus erogavit ; et ex hoc maximam multitudo pauperum ad eum confluxit ; quos ipse docuit habere voluntariam paupertatem, et esse imitatores Christi et Apostolorum. Cum autem esset aliquantulum litteratus, Novi Testamenti textum docuit eos vulgariter.

---

[20] Morland, "The History of the Evangelical Church of the Valleys of Piemont," London, 1658, page 25 ; John Leger, " Histoire des Eglises Evangeliques de Piemont," Amsterdam, 1669, pages 14, 15, 169 ; and a score of their imitators, copyists, and followers.

[21] Robyn, in his "Histoire de Lyon," confirms this statement, saying (page 268) that Peter Valdo homme grand riche, le quel estant sans mle sur sa porte avec ses voisins que prendre le frais . . . un de la trouppe tumbea subita raide mort sur la place, etc.

in their vernacular language." (Supply here what we know
from other contemporaries, that Peter had the Gospels translated by the two Priests Bernard Ydros and Steven de Ansa,
and that he and his followers went about preaching and
spreading errors.) "Being reproved for this act of temerity,
he treated the admonition with contempt, and obstinately
continued teaching, saying to his disciples that the Clergy,
living a wicked life, envied their holy life and doctrine.
The Pope then pronounced a sentence of excommunication
against them, but they stubbornly disregarded it. And
thus, to the present time, in every way they go on with
their doctrine and with their rancour."

SECTION VI.

PETER DE PILICHDORFF'S AUTHORITY.

ETER DE PILICHDORFF, S.T.P., wrote his
book against the Waldenses at the end of the fourteenth century, as appears from the thirtieth chapter of his treatise, where he says, that it was then the year of
our Lord thirteen hundred and ninety-five: "*Jam sicut scri-
bitur anno Domini* MCCCXCV." There are three manuscripts
of his work. The first[a] is entitled, "Oblationes contra Hœre-
ticos Valdensium." The second,[b] "Obviationes Sacræ Scripturæ contra Errores Baldenses." The third[c] has the full
title, "Petri de Pilichdorf Sacræ Theologiæ Professoris
contra Hæresim Valdensium Tractatus." (See Bibl. Patr.
tom. xxv. p. 277, *et seq.*) John Leger, in his "Histoire

---

*Pro qua temeritate cum fuisset reprehensus, contempsit et cœpit insidere doctrinæ
suæ, dictis discipulis suis, quod Clerus, quando male vixit sunt, insideret sanctæ
vitæ ipsorum et doctrinæ. Cum autem Papa excommunicationis sententiam tulisset
in eos, pertinaciter contempserunt. Et sic usque hodie in omnibus terminis illis
proficit doctrina ipsorum et rancor.*

---

[a] Desurdis MS.   [b] Nisobiana MS.   [c] Tegernsea MS.

Generale des Eglises Evangeliques de Piemont," at pages 20
and 175, and many other writers on the Waldenses, quote a
passage from a fragment of Pilichdorff detached from its
context, in order to confirm by it the fabulous antiquity of
the Waldenses; as the same Leger and some of his followers
are in the habit of doing with the authorities of several old
writers on the same subject. The time at which the Waldensian sect began is already undoubtedly proved by the
contemporaries in the first five articles, and in the fourteenth
article of this part will be established by an unanswerable
evidence from the ancient Waldensian manuscripts. I shall,
however, state here and in the next sections some of the
principal passages unfaithfully quoted by Morland, Leger
and their followers, to show that the historical truth is
actually confirmed by the authority of these very writers,
who, either through ignorance or malice, have been too often
quoted against it. Let us first read the whole text of
the Pilichdorff fragment as it is printed. (" Bibl. Patr." L. C.
p. 300).

" If the Waldenses should say that they are sent, let them
bring forward some proof of their mission, and say if they
have been sent by God or by any man. They are not sent by
God, because, in order to prove their mission, they say [a] that
a companion of Silvester in the time of Constantine would
not consent that the Church be enriched in those times, and
that he for this reason separated from Silvester, keeping the
path of poverty; and that the Church remained with him
and his followers who lived in poverty; and that Silvester
and his followers apostatized from the Church. Again, they

---

*Si Valdenses dicunt se missos, dicant suæ missionis testimonium, et an sint missi
a Deo vel ab homine. Non a Deo ; qui pro suæ missionis initio (alibi indicio) dicunt
quod socius Silvestri, tempore Constantini, noluit consentire quod Ecclesia Constantini temporibus ditaretur : et ex hoc a Silvestro recessit, viam proprietatis tenendo ;
apud quem etiam, suis adhærentibus in proprietate degentibus, Ecclesia permansit ;
et Silvestrum cum suis adhærentibus ab Ecclesia dicit cecidisse. Item quod post*

[a] Mark this well, " they say."

say that three" (say eight)[x] "hundred years after Constantine some one came out from the country of Waldis," called Peter, who equally taught the path of poverty, from whence the Waldensian sect sprung up. But what kind of wonderful signs are there to give testimony to these assertions? While on the contrary, the most famous actions and wonders of Silvester are known throughout the world." (Bibl. Patr. L. C. p. 278.)

Chapter the First. "The birth and Origin of the Waldensian heretics is this. Notwithstanding that the sons of iniquity are spreading falsehoods among simple people, saying that their sect lasted from the time of Pope Silvester, namely, when the Church began to have possessions of her own. The heretics think that this is not lawful, as the Apostles of Christ were commanded to live without any possession of their own. ' Do not possess gold or silver,' &c. The Church answers, that the same Lord Jesus Christ who whilst in his mortal body said so to his Disciples, yet at the time of his going out and parting from them, he said (Luke xxii.), ' But now he that has a purse, let him take it, and likewise a scrip.' What he forbade at first, he did allow them afterwards. It is therefore allowed to the Prelates of the Church to have possessions of their own to defend the Church, &c.

annos[x] ferentur a Constantino surrexit quidam e regione Waldis Petrus nominatus, qui similiter viam paupertatis docuit, a quibus secta Waldensis est orta. Sed quae signa virtutum praedictis prohibet testimonium? cum tamen facta celeberrima et miracula Silvestri totum mundum non latuerunt.

Caput 1.—Ortus et origo haereticorum Waldensium talis est. Licet iniquitatis filii corum simplicibus mentiuntur dicentes, sectam eorum durasse a temporibus Silvestri Papae, quando videlicet Ecclesia coepit habere proprias possessiones. Huc haereviarcha reputant non licere, cum Apostoli Christi vitae proprio jussi sint vivere. (Matth. x.): Nolite possidere aurum neque argentum, etc. Respondet Ecclesia, quod idem Dominus Jesus Christus, qui quamvis vermait in corpore mortali dixit ad discipulos verbum praemissum; ipso tempore recessus et separationis ab eis dixit (Luca xxii.): Sed nunc qui habet sacculum tollat similiter et peram. Quod prius prohibuit, postea concessit. Ideo licet Prelatis Ecclesiasticis habere proprium ad

* This three is a mistake of the transcriber. It must be eight hundred years, as the same author says, in the text passage, and as we shall see it also stated in the Wal-

densian manuscripts.
[x] Vaud or Vaux, in Latin Valdem, by the Elbert, near Lyons.

Then they (the Waldenses) state a falsehood when they say
that their sect lasted from the time of Pope Silvester.
Wherefore, it is to be marked, that about eight hundred years
after Pope Silvester, at the time of Innocent II.,[a] in the
town of Walden, which is situated on the frontier of France,
there was a certain rich citizen, who either read himself, or
heard that the Lord said to a youth (Matth. xix.), 'If thou
wilt be perfect, go sell what thou hast, and give it to the
poor.' And as he went away sad, because he was rich and
possessing much property, the Lord said, that ' A rich man
shall hardly enter into the Kingdom of Heaven.' And again,
' It is easier for a camel to pass through the eye of a needle
than for a rich man to enter into the Kingdom of Heaven.'
And after a few words, Peter said to the Lord, ' Behold, we
have left all things and have followed thee.' Hearing or
reading this passage of Scripture, that Peter Waldensis
taught that the Apostolic life was no more on earth, and
resolved to renew it; and selling everything he had and
giving it to the poor, began to lead a life of poverty. Some
other persons seeing this, were touched in their hearts, and
did the same. . . . . Having been a length of time in
poverty, they began to consider that the Apostles were not

*defensionem Ecclesiam, &c. . . . Mentiuntur ergo quod se tempore Silvestri Papæ
secta eorum duraverit. Unde notandum est[10] quod fere octingentis annis post
Papam Silvestrum, tempore Innocentii Papæ II., in civitate Walden, quæ in finibus
Franciæ sita est, fuit quidam civis dives, qui vel ipse legit vel audivit Dominum
dixisse cuidam adulescenti (Matth. xix.): Si vis perfectus esse, vade, vende omnia
quæ habes et da pauperibus. Et cum ille tristis abiisset, eo quod dives fuerat multas
possessiones habens, dixit Dominus : Quia dives difficile intrabit in regnum cælorum.
Et iterum : Multo facilius est camelum per foramen acus transire quam divitem
intrare in regnum cælorum. Et post pauca dixit Petrus Domino : Ecce nos
reliquimus omnia et secuti sumus te. Putabat ille Petrus Waldensis, cum hunc
audiret aut legeret scripturam, quod vita Apostolica jam non esset in terra. Unde
cogitabat eam innovare ; et omnibus venditis et pauperibus datis, cepit vitam pau-
perem ducere. Quod videntes quidam alii, corde compuncti sunt et fecerunt similiter . . . Cum autem diu in paupertate fuissent, inceperunt cogitare quod dum*

[a] As Innocent II. was Pope from the year
1130 till 1143, we must say either that the
author speaks here of the time in which

Peter Waldensis was a youth, or that the
manuscript was incorrect, or badly copied.

only poor, but preachers also. And they too began to preach the Word of God. Their manner of acting being reported to the Apostolic See, the Apostolic Lord commanded them to desist, because the preaching of the Word of God was not becoming for ignorant and unlearned people. They refused to obey, under the pretext that the Roman Court issued that prohibition moved by envy. As soon as it was known, the Church excommunicated them. And as they resisted with stubbornness, they were condemned by the Church; and as they did not venture to preach publicly, they preached privately. Then in hatred of the Clergy and of the true Priesthood, assuming the errors of old heretics, and adding new and dangerous articles, they began to destroy everything, except the Sacraments only; and to condemn and blame those practices by which the Clergy, as a pious mother, unite their children, as the hen gathers her little ones under her wings. . . . . And having so preached secretly for a long time, and under the appearance of fictitious godliness having detached many from the communion of the faithful, and brought them to their sect; they thought their preaching ineffectual, unless they also scrutinized the consciences of their followers, through hearing their Confessions. And after a time, they began at last to hear Confessions, to enjoin penances, and absolve from

---

Apostoli Christi non solum erant pauperes, imo etiam prædicatores; ceperunt et ipsi prædicare Verbum Dei. Quod postquam ad Sedem Apostolicam pervenisset, mandat Dominus Apostolicus quod cessarent, cum prædicatio verbi Dei rudibus et illiteratis non conveniret. Ipsi noluerunt obedire, quasi hoc Romana Curia ex invidia prohibuerit. Quo comperto Ecclesia excommunicavit eos. Et ipsi resistentes contumaciter, ab Ecclesia condemnati sunt. Et quia jam in publico prædicare non præsumebant, occulte multos prædicabant. Unde, in odium Clericorum et veri Sacerdotii, ex antiquis erroribus cæterorum hæreticorum et superadditis novis et damnosis articulis, incœperunt, solis exceptis Sacramentis, omnia destruere et condemnare et reprobare, per quæ Clerus, velut pia mater, filios congregat, sicut gallina congregat pullos suos sub alis. . . Cum enim longo tempore prædicassent taliter, et multos, sub prætextu sanctitatis apparentis simulationis, a fidelium communione ad sectam retam abduxerint; cogitabant inutiles esse ipsorum prædicationes, nisi etiam scrutarentur conscientias credentium suorum per Confessiones. Tandem post successum temporis, incœperunt Confessiones audire, pœnitentias injungere, et a peccatis absolvere. Et quia credentes ipsorum viderent et quotidie viderent eos

sins." And because their followers saw and daily see them
endowed with an exterior godliness, and a good many Priests
of the Church (O shame!) entangled with vices, chiefly of
lust, they believe that they are better absolved from sins
through them than through the Priests of the Church. And
if the Mercy of God be not pleased to inspire the Prelates of
the Church to be more vigilant, there is fear that they may
usurp for themselves still greater power."

SECTION VII.

ARCHBISHOP SEYSSELL'S EVIDENCE.

JOHN LEGER, in his history of the Evangelical
Churches, quotes (at pages 15 and 171) amongst
others a passage of the Rev. Claudius Seyssell,
Archbishop of Turin, endeavouring to prove the fabulous
Origin of the Waldensian sect by the authority of so good a
witness; and making him say, that it arose in the time of
the Great Constantine, from a very holy man called Leo. I
shall give here the full text of Seyssell alluded to, from
which it will appear, that if Leger be not a deceiver, certainly
he was grossly deceived. Archbishop Seyssell had the
people of the valleys of Piemont under his pastoral jurisdiction, and visited them carefully in their villages and houses.
It cannot be imagined then that he knew less of the Waldenses of his time and their history than Perrin, Morland,
Leger, and others, who spoke of them at a later age.
Seyssell wrote his forcible and elegant disputations "Ad-

---

exteriori sanctitate pallere, Sacerdotes vero Ecclesiæ quamplures in vitiis, proh dolor! et maxime carnalibus insistere, credunt se melius per eos a peccatis absolvi posse, quam per Sacerdotes Ecclesiæ. Et nisi Divina Clementia disponat fuerit Prælatis Ecclesiæ majorem inspirare vigilantiam, timendum est ne forte majorem sibi adhuc usurpent potestatem.

" Though this last part of the document   I have inserted it here to shew the reader how
does not bear directly on the present subject,   far an fair a writer is to be treated.

versus errores et sectam Valdensium," at the beginning of
the sixteenth century. I shall produce a few passages from
the edition of Paris, MDXX., hoping that the reader will not
be tired with seeing the same facts repeated many times,
and in so many documents. The Origin of the Waldenses
has been for more than two centuries so much darkened
with clouds of artificial misstatements by a great many
writers, that, in order to establish the truth, it is necessary
to bring forward many more witnesses than would be the
case with regard to an ordinary historical fact.

"(Sheet I.) The weed of which we have resolved to speak,
is the heresy of the Waldenses, who by the Roman Church
are commonly called *The Poor of Lyons.* (Sheet II.) There
is confided to me the country in which the infection of this
plague either began or has obstinately endured from the
beginning of the sect to this time. It is more than two
hundred years* since this heresy has been propagated in
our diocese of Turin, principally in its extreme parts and
amongst the gorges of those Alps, which divide France
from Italy, both in the royal dominions of Dauphiny and
those of Savoy: and the same sect has also in our age been

(Fol. I.) *Hoc autem, de quo loqui decrevimus sinimis, heresis est Valdensium,
quos Pauperes de Lugduno Ecclesia Romani vulgo appellat . . . (Fol. II.) Est
en mihi regio creditis in qua pestis hujus lues vel initium fecit, vel ab ipsa sectæ
origine vel hac usque tempora obstinatissime peraceverit. Quippe in hac Tauri-
nensi Diæcesi nostra, in extremis prouncia ejus partibus et inter ipsas Alpium quas
Galliam ab Italia determinant fauces, tam in regia Delphinalique quam in Sabau-
dicnsi ditione, supra cætera dæcvitus hæc hærresis inualuit, polemque unumrumquam*

---

* Mark the words: *It is more than two
hundred years since this heresy has been propagated in our diocese of Turin, amongst the
gorges of those Alps which divide France
from Italy.* This statement baffles the as-
serters of the immemorial existence of the
Vaudois in Piemont. Archbishop Seyssell
wrote his disputations certainly not later
than the year 1519, when he died. Let us
allow that the words, more than two hundred
years, may mean any additional period of
years less than one hundred, because the expression, more than two hundred years, could
not thus be exact; the author ought to have
said, in this case, it is near about three hundred years. Yet let us allow, for the sake
of argument, that the time meant by the
said expression be three hundred years before
the death of Seyssell. Now, deducting 300
from 1519, we have 1219 as the farthest ap-
proximate year in which the Waldensian
heresy could have existed in Piemont. In
Section XII. of this first part the reader will
find a more positive proof to the same
point.

not unfrequently defended by the inhabitants, both by arms
and by public disputations and preaching. (Sheet V.) Now
in order to come to the point, it is proper to mention the
Origin of this sect, in order that everybody may know that
it did not proceed from a man in any way famous; because
its author, whosoever he was, had so low an extraction, and
so little learning and reputation, that his very disciples do
not dare to mention his name publicly: and as regards either
holiness of life, or literary pursuits and virtues and miracles,
he had no renown at all. He was celebrated on this account
only, that he gave his name to a very dangerous and impious sect. It is said that he was called Waldonsis, and
that he had the freedom of the town of Lyons, from whence
the infection of this plague spread. Nevertheless,[a] some
patrons of this heresy, in order to obtain favour with
common persons ignorant of history, tell the story, that
this sect had its beginning at the time of Constantine the
Great, from a certain Leo, a man of very great sanctity,
who holding in abhorrence the covetousness of Silvester,
then the Pontiff of the city of Rome, and the boundless
prodigality of the same Constantine, preferred following
poverty in the simplicity of his faith to being defiled with

ab incolis et armis et publicis disceptationibus concionibusque, nostro etiam aetate,
defensa fuit. . . (Fol. V.) Primus igitur (ut ad rem ipsam accedamus) Originem
sectae hujus ex ratione commemorare concrevit, ut intelligant omnes, non ab alicujus
nominis viro praemisse. Hic denim qualiscunque fuerit, tam obscuro loco ortus,
tamque tenuina doctrina tenlinaque existimationis fuit, ut ne ipsi quidem ejus
discipuli primam proferre audeant: utpote qui neque vitae sanctitate neque literarum
scientia neque virtutum et miraculorum gloria clarus, hac solo nomine famosus extitit,
quod perniciosissimae impiissimaeque sectae ex suo nomine vocabulum indidit. Valdensis quippe (ut aiunt) appellabatur, et Lugdunensis urbis municeps fuit, unde et
primo hujus pestis contagio pullulavit. (Confirmatur fabula ficti auctoris.) Quamvis
nonnulli hujus haeresis assertores, ut blandiendum apud vulgares et historiarum
ignaros favorem, hanc extram sectam Constantini Magni temporibus, a Leone quodam
viro religiosissimo, initium sumpsisse fabulentur, qui, accerata Silvestri Romanae
urbis tunc Pontificis avaritia, et Constantini ipsius immoderata largitione; paupar-
tatem in fidei simplicitate sequi maluit, quam cum Silvestri pinqui opulentisque
fraterdotia contaminari. Cui cum amare, qui de Christiana religione recte senti—

[a] Here, at the margin, is printed, "The fable of the forged author is refuted."

the rich and earthly Priesthood of Silvester; (Sheet VI.)
and that all those who were rightly affected to the Christian
Religion, having united with Leo, and living according to
the rule of the Apostles, transmitted this rule of true
Religion to posterity. What can be more fabulous than this
falsehood? Amongst so many approved Greek and Latin
writers, who lived at that time or afterwards, who is there
that has mentioned this man (Leo)? while there is left an
everlasting memory of Antony, of Hilary and other ancho-
rites, who, besides abandoning all worldly goods, passed their
lives in the vast wilderness. From this single argument it
is made clear that this heresy had its Origin not from that
Leo, or from any other man famous for doctrine and holiness, but from that very citizen of Lyons, called Waldensis.
He with perverted texts of the Holy Scriptures, and with
sanctity simulated under the garb of poverty, having persuaded simple and unlearned men and women to adopt his
own opinions; spread in that town and the neighbourhood
errors not a few, under the pretext of teaching a new
religion. Afterwards (as the inconstancy of men is eager
for novelties) the number of his followers being greatly
increased, and the heresy of their opinions having become
evident, he with his disciples was sent into exile from
Lyons. The greatest number of them took refuge in the
neighbouring mountains, hoping, not without reason as the

*hood, adhæsissent, sub Apostolorum regula circates (Fol. VI.) hæc per manus
ad posteros reræ religionis normam transmiserunt. Quo sane commento quid potest
esse fabulosius? Quis enim est inter tot probatos auctores Græcos et Latinos, qui
per id tempus vel deinceps extitere, qui hujus hominis fecerit mentionem? Quum
tamen Antonii, Hilarii, cæterorumque anachoritarum, qui præter rerum omnium
humanarum contemptum, arctissimam in vasta solitudine ritum degerunt, memoria
relicta sit sempiterna. Quo uno argumento fit perspicuum, non a Leone illo aliove
ullius nominis doctrinæ sanctitatisque viro; sed ab ipso Lugdunensi cive Valdensi
nomine, hæresim hanc initium sumpsisse. Hic ampæ, simplicibus et indoctis tam
viris tum feminæ mulierculis, adulteriniis Sacræ Scripturæ doctrinis et simulata sub
paupertatis specie sanctitate, in suas sententias persuasis, errores nonnullos sub
novæ religionis prætextu, in ea urbe vicinisque locis disseminare cœpit. Deinde (ut
est hominum inconstantia novarum rerum cupida) aucto majorem in modum sancta-
torum numero et patefacta hæresi, Lugduno cum suis sequacibus pulsus, in proxima
montana horum pars maxima sunt delapsi, haud imrigicaanter sperantes, quod cæratus

event showed, that amongst country people labouring under
the want of worldly goods, and still more of learning and
Religion, it would be easy to persuade them to adopt principles, which, besides being pleasant in themselves, could
without trouble be accepted by ignorant persons, when confirmed by some kind of reasons and some authority of the Holy
Scripture. . . . The poison began to spread gently . . . and
by-and-by some persons of some learning, but already badly
disposed against our Religion, or for some cause enemies to
the Priests, through opposition and envy, began to be united
to the sect. . . . (Sheet LXXXIX.) At last, to put an end
to our volume, I pray you, O simple and unlearned men,
whosoever have been deceived by these barbas and heretics,
I pray you by the power of Almighty God . . . and for
the salvation of your souls, I exhort and conjure you to be
on your guard against these false prophets, who approach
you in the dress of sheep, but inwardly are ravening wolves.
. . . Who forged some genealogies of that holy Leo, who
never existed, from whom as we have said, they falsely
state that in the age of the Great Constantine their sect had
its origin, and that in subsequent times others succeeded
him."

---

docuit, fore ut rusticanæ plebis, inopiæ rerum multæque magis ingeniorum et doctrinæ Religionisque laboranti, ea facile persuaderet quæ, præterquam quod conspicuibilea essent pro sese, ratione insuper aliqua et auctoritate Sacræ Scripturæ, apud imperitum vulgus approbari haud gravate possent. . . Venenum paulatim diffundi cœpit. Donec prædictim nonnulli alicujus literaturæ viri, sed iam jampridem de nostra Religione male sentientes, aut Sacerdotibus aliquo ex causa infensi, ad æmulationem invidiamque illorum, huic sectæ adhærere cœperunt. (Fol. LXXXIX.) Denique, ut finem imponamus operi, vos o simplices et ignari litterarum, quicunque ab his barbis et hæreticis decepti estis, per Omnipotentis Dei virtutem . . . et per salutem animarum vestrarum, hortamur et obsecramus, ut ab istis falsis prophetis caveatis, qui veniunt ad vos in vestimentis ovium, intrinsecus autem sunt lupi rapaces. . . . Qui genealogias quasdam conflagrant illius s. Leonis, qui nunquam fuit, a quo tempore Constantini Magni sectam hanc, ut prædiximus, initium habuisse et alios illi per tempora successisse, mentiuntur.

SECTION VIII.

ENEAS SYLVIUS PICCOLOMINI'S STATEMENT.

HERE are some other authors to be quoted, not because their authority is necessary to confirm what is already proved by the testimony of so many contemporaries, but because they are brought forward by John Leger, as holding the fabulous antiquity of the Waldenses, whilst it evidently appears that they are all against it. Eneas Sylvius Piccolomini, afterwards Pius II. (1458) is the first in order of time. His authority quoted by Leger (L. C. page 172) does not prove anything for him. Piccolimini, speaking of the Waldenses, says that they were *a pestilent faction long ago condemned. Une faction pestilente et de long tens condemnée.* Considering the date at which the Waldenses were first condemned, namely about sixteen years[*] before the end of the twelfth century; and the time in which Eneas Sylvius wrote his Bohemian History, namely about the middle of the fifteenth century, every body will perceive that the expression "*long ago*" cannot be used to prove for the Waldensian sect any greater antiquity than the real one of about two centuries and a half before the time in which Piccolomini wrote his history. The passage (Æneæ Sylvii "Opera quæ extant omnia." "Historia Bohemica," cap. 35, p. 103, Basileæ, 1571) is this :

"They (the followers of Wickliff) broke forth into blasphemies, and began to clamour against all Priests; and retiring from the Catholic Church, gave their names to the impious and foolish Waldensian sect. The doctrines of this pestilent faction long ago condemned are these," &c.

---

[*] *Prorumpunt in blasphemias et . . . in omnes latrare Sacerdotes corperunt, et ab Ecclesia Catholica recedentes, impiam Valdensium sectam atque insaniam compleri sunt. Hujus pestiferæ ac jam pridem damnatæ factionis dogmata sunt,* etc.

---

[*] By Pope Lucius III., the year 1184. (See our note 8.)

Section IX.

SAMUEL CASINI'S EVIDENCE.

HE second in order of time is Samuel Casini or de Casinis, who by the same J. Leger (I. C. p. 15) is made to say that the Waldenses are as old as the Christian Church: and the same Leger (I. C. 172) assures us that Casini says that he *for his part cannot deny that the Waldenses always had been and still were members of the Christian Church.* I could not find in the principal libraries of England or Italy Casini's *Vittoria Triomfale* quoted by Leger (L. C.). But I have found in the King's Library of Turin, a little Latin volume of the same author, printed in the same year 1550, and at the same place (Cuneo) as mentioned by Leger, in which the same argument is treated; but the expressions are quite contrary to those stated by Leger. The book begins thus: *De statu Ecclesiæ, De Purgatorio, De Suffragiis Defunctorum, De Corpore Christi. Libellus feliciter incipit contra Valdenses qui hæc omnia negant.* At the end of the volume there is printed: *Perfectus est iste tractatulus per me Fratrem Samuelem de Casinis die 26 Octobris* 1510 *die Sabbati in mane. Impressum autem per me Simonem Bevilaqua Papiensem in egregio oppido Cunei anno nostræ salutis* 1510. Let us hear what he says on the point.

"These (pp. 2, 3) are the arguments of the Waldenses, in their substance extracted by myself from their sayings, from which it clearly appears, that *they conclude,* that they are the Church of God, and that the real Pope is amongst them. The truth is manifestly the reverse; because what they say cannot be proved by any direct or indirect authority of the

Ista sunt argumenta Valdensium virtualiter ex suis dictis a me excerpta, ex quibus clare patet ipsos inferre quod ipsi sunt Ecclesia Dei, et quod in ipsis est verus Papa. In contrarium patet veritas, eo quod ex nullo inductorie Scripturæ, neque directe neque

Holy Scripture, and besides it is repugnant to all reason.
. . . . From what (*five pages before the end*) has been said,
after a sufficient division, it follows that the barbarians and
the Jews, who evidently are infidels, or the Valdenses who
do not know the Church of God, and who deny the practices
of the Church of God, which she now holds, and has received
from the primitive Church, are not the Church of God."

Section X.

REV. EDMUND CHAMPION'S ASSERTION.

HE third, in order of time, is the famous Edmund
Champion, S. J., who towards the end of his life
in London, gave in his little pamphlet an eloquent
and forcible account of his own Catholic persuasion to the
English " Academicians." A passage of his also is grossly
misrepresented by John Leger, who says (L. C. p. 15),
that Champion calls the Waldenses *Majores nostros*, and
from this appellation argues that Champion means to say
that the Waldenses are more ancient than the Church of
Rome. And the same Leger repeating again (L. C. p. 171)
the *Majores nostros* as said by Edmond Champion, adds sati-
rically: " Yes your Majora, from whom you have much
degenerated," *Dont vous avez bien degeneré.* Now let us
read the only passage in the Address of Champion* to which
Leger can possibly have alluded, and mark either the ignorance or the impudence of this undeservedly celebrated
historian of the Waldenses.

---

indirecte potest hoc dici, imo repugnat omni rationi. . . Ex dictis ergo (probatur)
a sufficienti divisione, non esse Ecclesiam Dei barbaros et Judeos qui reprobant sunt
infideles, nec Valdenses qui ignorat Ecclesiam Dei, et qui negant eandem Ecclesiam
Dei, quam nunc tenet et habet a primitiva Ecclesia."

---

* " Prescriptionum adversus hereticos: Ed-
mundi Campiani Rationes reddita Acade-
miciis Angliae—Secunda ratio," pages 670,
671, Moguntiae, anno MDCII.

"If the heretics should wish to have a Church, they are
obliged to establish one in the darkness, and call by the
name of their fathers those whom they had not known, and
no mortal man had ever seen. If perchance they would not
glory to acknowledge for their ancestors those who were
evidently heretics, as Aerius, Jovinianus, Vigilantius, Helvidius, the Iconoclasts, Berengarius, the Waldenses, Lo-
tharius, Wickleff, Huss, from whom they have begged
some fragments of doctrine."

SECTION XI.

PRIOR RORENGO'S TESTIMONY.

THERE are two other Catholic writers of the
middle of the seventeenth century, quoted by
Morland, Leger, and a great number of their
abettors, in order to confirm by some detached passages
stolen from them the immemorial antiquity of the Waldensian sect. The first is the Reverend Mark Aurelius
Rorengo, or Rorenco, of the Counts of Lucerna, one of the
Waldensian valleys. Sir James Morland ("History of the
Evangelical Churches of the Valleys of Piemont." London,
1658, pp. 13 to 28,) and principally John Leger ("Histoire
Generale." Amsterdam, 1680, pp. 14, 163, 173,) quoting
Rorengo with praise, makes him say generally that "There
is no certainty of the time in which the Waldenses first
appeared, that in the ninth and tenth century they were
not a new sect," &c. We only observe that Rorengo speaking of the different sects of the eighth, ninth, tenth and

---

" *Hi (Hæretici) coguntur Ecclesiam, si quam volent, in latebris tradituri, et eos
patronos asserere, quos nec ipsi noverint, neque mortalium quisquam aspexerit.
Nisi forte pudeat nec oribus illis quos hæreticos fuisse liquet, ut Aerio, Joviniano,
Vigilantio, Helvidio, Iconomachis, Berengario, Waldensibus, Lutheanio, Wiclefo,
Hussio, a quibus pestiferi quorundam fragmenta dogmatum emendicarunt.*"

D

eleventh centuries, makes no mention of the Waldenses, or
the Poor of Lyons. When he mentions the twelfth century,
he points out that the Waldenses were condemned in that
century. But let us hear the Reverend Prior speaking for
himself, and destroying the castle built in the air.[m]

"They of the valleys, in order to show that they are
of an ancient source, put forward and boast to be the
descendants of Waldus. . . . Now, Boterus relates, that
from the year 1159, Waldus began to form a new doctrine
in Lyons, and that he retired with his disciples into the
valleys and Alps of the Dauphiny and Provence, and that
some others went to Picardy. Gualterius says, that this fact
happened in the year 1160, and that Waldus was condemned at the Council of the Lateran under Pope Alexander.[n] . . . Now there are persons who say that out of
those who were exiled from Lyons, there were some who
from that very time retired to the valley of Angrogna.
But I believe that they only stopped within the mountains
of Dauphiny, because there is no proof either that they

_Questi delle valli si vogliono e si vorrano di esarre delli discendenti di Valdo
. . . Ora il Batero riferisce che del 1159 cominciò l'oldo a formarsi una nuova
dottrina in Lione, e che in poco tempo sia stato cacciato da Lione, e ritiratosi con i
suoi nelle valli e Alpi del Delfinato e Proenza, altri in Piccardia. Gualterio dice
che fosse nel 1160, e che sia stato condannato nel concilio Lateranense sotto papa
Alessandro . . . Ora vi è chi vuole che di questi scacciati da Lione, chiamati
Valdesi o Poveri di Lione, se ne fossero sino in quelli tempi ritirati nella valle di
Angrogna. Ma credo che adunando si siano trattenuti nelli monti del Delfinato ;
poichè non si trova che abbino testimonio di alcun suo progresso, nè di giustizia i suoi_

[m] "Breve narrazione dell' introduzione
degli eretici nelle Valli del Piemonte," Torino
1832, pagro 47, 49, 50. And "Memoria
istoriche dell' introduzione dell'eresia nelle
Valli di Luserna &c." Torino, 1649. And
also "Esame intorno alla nuova Confessione
di fede delle Chiese riformate di Piemonte,"
Torino, 1856.

[n] This is Alexander the Third, who, exalted to the Popedom in 1159, held the third
Council of Lateran, which was the eleventh
general, in the year 1179, and died in 1181.
The assertion of Gualterius, that the Waldenses were condemned at the said Council,
is not confirmed, to my knowledge, by any
document. That some delegates of their

body went to Rome in order to be au-
thorised in their proceedings, and that they
went back with a refusal, is the only fact
ascertained by the English Franciscan Walter
Mapes or Mapens, who saw, and had some
conversation with two of them in Rome, and
has left a very interesting account about them
in his work, "De Nugis Curialium," kept
among the MSS. of the Bodleian Library,
Oxford. The part of the MS. in which is
related his conversation with two of the members, in his work "De Christianus, Ecclesias,
. . . Continues unrevenius," &c. Lansdini,
1687, f. 112.

came here, or that they suffered any punishment; but that many years afterwards, having much increased in numbers, they spread into different parts of the world. . . . So we cannot state with certainty the time in which they first came here. It is not very easy ("Mem. Istor." pp. 6 and 7) to find out precisely the time at which the Waldensian sect was introduced here, and what their belief was. Some persons thought that they were Albigenses already confuted in the time of Saint Dominic. . . . Others were of opinion that they were followers of John Huss and of Jerom of Praga. . . . But the common opinion is that they are disciples of Waldus, called Waldenses, or Poor of Lyons, who exiled from France, retired part into the corners of Provence, part into those Alps which stand between France and Piemont. They had this peculiarity, namely, to live in common, and to be very secret in their doctrines. . . . Besides, in order that their errors might not be there known, each one of them was ordered to attend publicly the Divine Services of the Catholics. . . . Now, without going from the proofs (Esame, p. 9), from the very assertions of your own writers, it is manifest that the opinion, of your ancestors having professed the Thirty-three Articles from the Apostles to our own time, is a false one. . . . Because though from that time to the present hour, there have been many sects, or, as you say, churches, adverse and rebellious to the Catholic

che molti anni dopo, essendo assai popolato, si sieno sparsi in molte parti del mondo . . . e così non si può aver contezza del principio del mio ingresso.

Il sapere precisamente il tempo che fu introdotta la setta dei Valdesi in questi popoli, e che cosa abbiamo creduto, non è tanto facile. Alcuni sono stati di parere che fossero Albigesi confutati fino al tempo di San Domenico . . . Altri li stimorono seguaci di Giovanni Huss e di Girolamo di Praga . . . Però la comune opinione è che siano dei seguaci di Valdo, chiamati Valdesi o Poveri di Lione, quali usciriti da Francia, si ritirarono parte in alcuni angoli della Provenza, ed altri fra quelle Alpi tra Francia e Piemonte. Ebbero questi in particolare il vivere in comune, e segretissimi nella dottrina. Anzi per non palesare allora i loro errori, ciascuno era trattato di andare publicamente alli Divini Officii Cattolici. . . . Ora, senza partire dalle prove, con vostri proprii scrittori consta che falsa sia l'opinione, cioè avere li vostri antenati professata la Confessione dei 33 articoli dalli Apostoli sino ai vostri ultimi tempi . . . Che abbene da quel tempo sinora vi siano state sette, o chiese, come voi dite, opponenti anzi ribelli dalla Chiesa Cattolica, istoria non si trova rappresentale che

Church; yet there is nowhere distinctly to be found in them the confession of the Thirty-three Articles published by you. . . . (L. C. pp. 14 and 15.) I have represented all these facts in order to prove clearly that it is untrue that your confession of faith has been professed from the Apostles to this present age; because, there would have been found different practices, different orders, different articles, without making these new ones in the year 1564. . . . To endeavour to send a date a thousand years and centuries back, is a malice deserving to be severely corrected. . . . According (L. C. p. 47) to Saint Augustin, the true Church is that which communicates with the Roman Pontiff, whose succession to Alexander VII. we are prepared to hear you say is not as well proved, as the succession of your Barba Martini from the Apostles is proved by the chronicles and the synods of the valleys: the catalogues of which we are always expecting with great desire that you should show to us: because to the present time we could not obtain from you even one authentic proof of your continued succession in your beautiful Waldensian nobleness."

---

sin stata in essere la confessione di 33 articoli che dato avete alla luce. . . . Tutti questi metodi ho rappresentato per far credere evidentemente non esser vero che la vostra confessione di fede nuova sia stata professata dagli Apostoli sino a' nostri secoli, perchè si sarebbero già ritrovate altre discipline, altre ordinanze, altri articoli senza fare questi nuovi nel 1564 . . . l malizia da esser corretta con severità. Vera è la Chiesa che comunica col Pontefice Romano, dice Sant' Agostino; la di cui successione sino ad Alessandro VII. siccome aspettando che mi alleghiate esser non provata che quella degli Apostoli sino alli vostri Barba Martini, per le croniche e sinodi delle valli; delle quali siccome con gran desiderio attendiamo che voi facciate vedere i cataloghi, mentre sino ad ora non abbiamo da voi potuto ritrarre una prova autentica della continuata vostra della nobiltà Valdese.

Section XII.

REV. THEODORUS BELVEDERE'S EVIDENCE.

HE Reverend Theodorus Belvedere is the other author alluded to in Sect. xi. Morland (l. c. pp. 28, 37), Leger (l. c. pp. 14, 109), and others, quote the following passage from Belvedere's "Relazione all' Eṁa Congregazione di Propaganda Fede" (Torino, 1636): "The valley of Angrogna always and in every time had heretics." And the reader is directed by them hence to conclude, that this "famous missionary" (as Leger calls him) confirms the supposed immemorial antiquity of the Waldensian sect. Now, let us read the full text of Theodorus, and it will be evident that his assertion does not extend the antiquity of the sect further than the time of Peter Waldensis. Besides the passages from the "Relazione," I shall give some other extracts from the same author out of his "Turris contra Damascum," also printed at Turin in the same year, 1636, which will confirm the same point.

"('Relazione,' p. 37.) Further to the North, facing the West, there is the valley of Angrogna, which at one time or another always had heretics, either Albigenses or Waldenses, as is gathered from the chronicle of the Dominican Fathers, where it is stated that the holy Vincent Ferreri had been preaching there."[*] (P. 242, *et seq.*) "The unhappy valleys of Lucerna, Angrogna, Saint Martin, and Perosa . . . . always have been subject to various plagues of heretical

---

Più verso il settentrione ed medesimo aspetto occidentale è la valle di Angrogna, la quale sempre in un tempo o in un altro ha avuto eretici o Albigesi o Valdesi, secondo che si raccoglie dalle croniche dei Padri Domenicani, memorandoci esserci stato a predicare il Santo Vincenzo Ferreri. . . Le sfortunate valli di Lucerna, Angrogna, San Martino e Perosa . . . sempre sono state soggette a varii flagelli e

---

[*] Saint Dominic, the founder of the Dominican Order, died in the year 1221, and St. Vincent Ferreri much later, in the year 1419.

locusts, or of unfruitful caterpillars, mildew and grass-hoppers. Wherefore the most illustrious and most reverend Prior of Lucerna says, in his Narrative of the introduction of the heretics into the valleys of Piemont, that it was the opinion of some persons that the first heretics introduced into the valleys had been the Albigenses, who came out from the mouth of Cerberus about the year 1160." . . . . (*Ibid.* p. 249, *et seq.*) "And since the same Prior concludes, that he thinks it probable that the heretics now living in the said valleys are the descendants of Waldus, I may be allowed to explain in a few words the time at which they arose, who was their founder, and how they came into the valleys, and how they changed their sect, adopting the reformation of Calvin. According to Guido, they arose about the year of our Lord 1170, from Waldus merchant of Lyons, who, excited by the heresy of the Catharites, which was spreading at that time, rose up and caused a schism against the Roman Church." . . .

It would be useless to quote everything Belvedere says about the Waldenses in his Narrative, as the present point is to show that this writer, by the expression that "those valleys always had heretics," does not mean a time prior, but posterior, to the existence of Peter Waldensis. This clearly appears, not only from the reported passages, but is further shown from his quoting an order, dated the 28th November, 1474, "against the heretics of the valley of Lucerna, called Poor of Lyons," bearing the signature of John Campesio, Bishop of Turin, and of Father Andrew

di eretici di locuste, o d' infidi bruchi, rubigini e convallette. Onde narra il molto illustre e molto Reverendo Signor Priore di Lucerna nella sua narrazione della introduzione degli eretici nelle valli di Piemonte, essere stato parere di alcuni che i primi eretici in queste valli introdotti sieno stati Albigesi, i quali uscivano dalla fauci di Cerbero l'anno 1160 in circa. . . E perchè il medesimo Signor Priore conchiude, parere a lui verisimile che gli eretici che ora in dette valli dimorano sieno discendenti da Valdo, mi sia lecito con due parole esplicare il tempo che questi principiarono ; l'autore, e come vennero nelle valli, e come abbiano mutato setta col pigliare la riforma Calviniana. Questi, secondo Guido, ebbero principio circa l'anno del Signore 1170 da Valdo mercante di Lione, il quale cominciò a sollevarsi e fare scisma contro la Chiesa Romana, eccitato della eresia dei Cattori, che a quel tempo si promulgavano.

John of Acquapendente, Under-delegate of the Holy Office,
as well as from a proclamation of the Most Serene Duchess
Jane of Savoy, dated Rivoli, 23rd January, 1416, "against
the heretics, poor of Lyons or Waldenses," in order to prove
that the Waldenses were then in the valleys. But let us
hear Belvedere again in his "Turris contra Damascum" (pp.
26, 27, 30), where, besides repeating the fact of their being
founded by Peter Waldensis, he reproaches the sectarians
for having abandoned their mother the Catholic Church:

"The Waldenses are those who, being the followers of
Peter Waldone of Lyons, in France, were called at first the
Poor of Lyons. . . Since that Waldus of Lyons, their father
and founder, being a cunning and rich merchant, desiring to
found and assemble a new sect through the persuasion of
Satan, in order to comply with his licentiousness, resolved
to renew the old Church of the Apostles, in which everything was in common, principally the wealth. And so he
gave his riches in common, and a great many poor, who
were starving, gathered around him. From thence the sect
of the Poor of Lyons began. . . That the Waldenses afterwards had corroded the bosom of their mother, when, like
the dog Cerberus, they bark so badly against the Roman
Church, endeavouring to pluck out of her her soul and
bowels, as Nero with Agrippina his mother, I think that it
cannot be reasonably disputed. And that the Roman Church
was to them a very kind mother, it is not only true in some

" Cæterum Valdenses sunt qui a Petro Valdone in Galliis Lugdunesi exorti,
primum Pauperes de Lugduno sunt appellati. . . Quoniam Valdus ille Lugdunensis, eorum parens et auctor, cum callidus esset locupletesque mercator, intraciens
(suam dementis) novam sectam, ut suæ libidini satisfaceret, instituere et consinuare;
vetustam Apostolicamque Ecclesiam, in qua omnia communia, præsertim facultates,
suppeditaretur, renovandum constituit. Sicque opibus suis in commune erogatis,
quamplurimi pauperes qui inedia confciebantur, confugerunt ad eum . . . hincque
secta Pauperum de Lugduno iniberavit. . . Quod deinceps Valdenses corroserint
viscera matris, dum adeo contra Romanam Ecclesiam instar canis Cerberi oblatrant,
viden viscera animal et animum, Neronis instar erga suam matrem Agrippinam,
eruere; arbitror non posse oppositum jure deduci. At vero quod Ecclesia Romana
extiterit eis humanissima parens, est adeo verum quam quod verisimum; nam ex eo

measure, but in the very highest degree. Because Waldus was her son, and he and his first followers were fed and nourished with the milk of her Evangelical Doctrine, and he in the year of our Lord 1170 drew his impious sword against his own nurse."

Section XIII.

EXTRACTS FROM SOME MANUSCRIPTS IN THE KING'S LIBRARY OF TURIN.

IN the library of King Victor Emanuel in Turin, there is an unpublished manuscript in folio, numbered 169; which appears to have been written a little after the time at which John Leger published his "Histoire Generale." The title of the manuscript is: "Histoire veritable des Vaudois," without the name of the writer. That part of the MS. which relates the facts which happened in the second half of the seventeenth century, is very interesting, and we shall make use of it in our second part. Here we shall only give a faithful summary of what the diligent and truthful writer says about the Origin of the Waldenses in Piemont. And in order that every body be able to compare our abridgment with the original, the numbers of the pages of the said MS. shall be quoted.

(Pp. 4, 5.) " Peter Waldensis from being a rich merchant, changed his manners of living, and followed poverty at the sudden death of one of his companions in the year 1160 under Louis VII. king of France, and Pope Alexander III."[*] That Peter Waldensis was the founder of the sect of the

---

ortus est Valdus, ejusque lacte Evangelicæ Doctrinæ nutritus uan cum primis suis sectariis et aditus, anno Domini 1170, gladium iniquum contra propriam nutricem arripuit."

[*] He sat in the Pontifical Chair from 1159 to 1181, as we have before remarked (note 24).

Vaudois is stated also by John Dubravius, Bishop of Olmutz in his fourteenth book of the Bohemian history ('Prestannæ ex Officina Gualterii an. 1552'), where he says: The author of the sect is Peter Waldensis, a Gaulois by nation, of the town of Lyons, a silly, ignorant and unlearned man, who is not worthy to be numbered amongst the serious heretics. '*Auctor ejus Petrus cognomine Waldensis, natione Gallus, civitate Lugdunus, vir idiota, indoctus illiteratus, nec dignus inter serios hæreticos numerari.*' (P. 9.) At the time of the said Alexander III. a Gallican Council was held in the year 1176, under the presidency of Guilbert, Bishop of Lyons, who with the approbation of a great number of Bishops and Prelates condemned Peter Waldensis as a false prophet, hypocrite and enemy of God."

Here I would call attention to what is reported by some other contemporaries of Peter Waldensis, and is also asserted by the Rev. G. B. Semeria ("Storia della Chiesa Metropolitana di Torino," 1840), namely that another Archbishop of Lyons, called Bolismanis or Belismanus, condemned Peter Waldensis, and even exiled him with his followers from his diocese. Belismanis ruled the diocese of Lyons from the year 1182 to the year 1195.[*]

(Pp. 32, 33.) " It seems that the first coming of the Waldenses into Piemont was at the time of Philip Augustus King of France. They, after retiring to the mountains of Douphiny, multiplied to such an extent that in order to procure for themselves the necessaries of life, by degrees they crossed the mountains of Piemont and descended into the valleys of St. Martin and Lucerna in the commons of Angrogna, Villar, and Bobbio. This happened when Thomas I. Count of Savoy and Prince of Piemont was yet a minor, under the guardianship of the Marquis of Monferrato; and the Savoyards adhered to Pope Alexander III. and were against the Emperor Frederick surnamed Redbear. Thomas

* See our note 6.

having attained his majority was obliged to take part in
the wars of his time, and could not attend to what was
taking place in the mountains and valleys of Piemont, where
the Counts of Lucerna still exercised a great power. It then
so happened that the Waldenses had time to settle there and
to multiply with their families; and they were not molested
at that time by the Catholic inhabitants of the places. The
fact is that at the beginning the Waldenses; keeping their
religious opinions to themselves alone, and holding their
secret meetings now on the very tops of the mountains, now
in the grottoes, now in their low and dark huts; gave no outward sign of their disagreeing in any way from the Catholic
Doctrines. Besides, they appeared of a good moral and tem-
perate life, and lovers of hard work; and at the same time
they frequented the Catholic Churches and occasionally
approached to the Sacraments with the Catholics. And in
order not to give rise to any suspicion that they were under
the spiritual guidance of their own religious chiefs, they
gave them the not suspicious name of Barba; which in Piemontese tongue means uncle, and is given to the elders also
as a mark of respect; and they thus disguised the honour
shown to them under the pretext of relationship or of old age."
(P. 42.) "But at last, James, Bishop of Turin, perceiving that
the bad Waldensian and heretical grass had grown in the
middle of his Catholic field, wrote to, and also called on the
Emperor Otto, in order to obtain his imperial aid in exter-
minating the Waldenses from his diocese, as the Bishop of
Lyons had done.* This happened in the year 1209 or 1210.
James obtained his petition and was fully authorized to employ for the purpose even the imperial assistance. But, as
immediately afterwards disagreements arose between the
Emperor and Pope Innocent III., it seems that the Bishop of

---

* John Bernerio, in his "Storia della
Chiesa Metropolitana di Torino," 1840, adds,
from old documents, that the Bishop, in his
application to the Emperor, said: That

heretics going astray with errors, and infle x-
ible with obstinacy had recently crept into his
diocese. Mark the word recently.

Turin was unable to employ the means promised to him, and in consequence the Waldenses remained unmolested " (Pp. 48, 50.) " Under the same Innocent III. the Waldenses, with other heretics were condemned in the Council of Lateran." [*]

Here we shall subjoin some other particulars relating to the first Waldensian existence in Piemont, abridged from another manuscript, also existing in the King's Library of Turin, amongst *Miscellanea Patria*, Volume cxxii. The author of the MS. is Monsieur Vegezzi, a very exact and careful writer.

" The oldest public document in which the Waldenses are mentioned who came into the district of Pinerolo, is contained in the book of the Statutes of that town of the year 1220. There is set a fine of ten soldi upon any person who should give shelter or harbour to any of those innovators. Observe that according to the opinion of antiquarians, ten soldi of the money of that time are equal to about 280 francs or lire of the present French and Italian coins, a very heavy fine indeed. The said book of Statutes was published in Turin in the year 1602, with this title: 'Statutes and Orders given by the most illustrious Count, and by the Wisemen of Pinerolo during the year twelve hundred and twenty.' *Statuta et ordinamenta facta per illustrissimum Dominum Comitem et Sapientes Pinerolii currente millesimo ducentesimo vigesimo.* 'Again it is ordained that if any man or woman shall knowingly give harbour to any Waldensis man or woman within the district of Pinerolo, he or she shall pay the fine of ten soldi every time he or she shall so harbour them.' *Item statutum est quod siquis vel si qua hospitaretur aliquem vel aliquam Valdensem vel Valdensam, se sciente, in posse Pinerolii, dabit bannum solidorum decem quotiescunique hospitabitur.*"

From the said document it is plain that in the year 1220 the Waldenses were not resident or established in the district of Pinerolo, and that they brought with themselves the

---

[*] It was the twelfth General Council and the fourth of Lateran held in the year 1215.

name of Waldenses, with which they were already called
before entering there.   This is a proof against those partial
writers, who, being forced by the historical evidence to admit
that Peter Waldensis is the author of the Waldensian sect;
nevertheless, without any foundation, state and endeavour to
make us to believe that the followers of Peter, coming into
Piemont, united themselves with the Vaudois already from
time immemorial supposed to exist there." Idle tale of
story tellers!

The same MS. continues : " From the said year 1220 the
Waldenses are not mentioned in any way in the Piemontese
documents till the year 1334 in which the Prince William of
Acaja gave an order to Belangerus of Rorengo, and to Uretto
his nephew, who were the masters of Della Torre, and to the
other feudatories of the valleys of Pellice and Chisone. The
order directed them to put a stop *to the preachers of those new
doctrines already excommunicated in the year* 1332 *by Pope John
XXII.; because the said preachers would not cease nor desist
from preaching.*   After this order, there is a long silence
about the Waldenses in the State Memorials for nearly a
century and a half.   Then comes a Rescript of Duchess Io-
lunta, dated the 23rd January, 1476, and an order of Duke
Charles I. issued in the year 1484 for the purpose of re-
pressing the Waldenses, who would not desist from spreading
their new principles.   And it was necessary that the Prince
should send a good number of soldiers to subdue them.
At that time the Waldenses would have been scattered altogether, if the element Sovereign had not, upon their humili-
ation and begging pardon, been moved to compassion.   He
was satisfied with only levying a fine to defray the expenses
of the war.   From this year 1484 there is no public act in
the Piemontese Annals having relation to the Waldenses,
till the year 1535."

* Rev Muston's "History of the Evan-
gelical Church;" William Jones's "History
of the Waldenses," London, 1812, page 343;
W. H. Gilly, M.A., "A Narrative," &c.,
London, 1827, page 18; Alexis Muston, D.D.,
"The Israel of the Alps," Glasgow, 1857—
Introduction; and many others.

Section XIV.

OTHER AUTHORITIES NOT LIABLE TO SUSPICION, PRINCIPALLY THAT OF THE WALDENSIAN MANUSCRIPTS.

T may be objected against most of the documents already quoted, that nearly all the authors, contemporary or near to the time of Peter Waldensis, are Catholics by profession, and some of them very bitter enemies of the Waldenses: and of course it may be supposed that they have not published what they knew about the antiquity of the Origin of the sect, at least from the time of the Great Constantine, or at the very latest at the time of that famous Claudius of Turin in the beginning of the ninth century.

I answer, first. By those who make this objection no proof is alleged of the existence of this sect, either at the time of Constantine or of Claudius of Turin; their statements are not confirmed by any document or historical fact; they are merely gratuitous suppositions. In consequence we may here apply that old sentence of the schools: what is asserted without proof, we have the right to deny without bringing forth any proof: *Quod gratis asseritur, gratis negatur.*

I answer, secondly, that Father Moneta at Section ii., Reinerius Sacco at Sect. v., Pilichdorff at Sect. vi., and Archbishop Seyssell, quoted at Sect. vii., have already dispelled the first supposition that the Waldenses are the successors of that holy man called Leo, who separated from Pope Silvester at the time of Constantine. It is not proved that this good holy man existed at all, and if he had been in existence then, he had no reason for separating himself from Pope Silvester on account of the prodigality of Constantine towards him: because it is a clear falsehood that Constantine had given to the Pope the Italian States, or even the crown

of the Western Empire. This is as great a lie in history as
would be the assertion that the Great Constantine was one
of the Popes of Rome. About the Spaniard Claudius, who
in the first part of the ninth century was Bishop, not Archbishop, of Turin under Louis, son and successor of Charles
the Great, I only say that he had no followers in his hatred
against the Cross and the holy Images. Louis the Pious,
who caused him to be made a Bishop, not knowing that
Claudius was an Iconoclast; when he afterwards learned of
his destroying the sacred pictures and figures, directed
Jonas, Bishop of Orleans, Agobert, Bishop of Lyons, and
Wilfridus, called Strabon, to write against and to condemn
the error and the doings of Claudius. Dungalius also, an
eloquent Deacon of the time, confuted his false opinions. I
cannot refrain from quoting a few lines of the last-mentioned
writer. (See Bibl. Patr. tom. XIV. p. 197, et seq.): "*Qualis et
quanta est insana elatio et vana temeritas, ut quod a primaevo
tempore Christianitatis per annos ferme* DCCCXX. *et eo amplius a
sanctis et beatissimis Patribus et religiosissimis postea Principibus* . . . *in Ecclesiis et in quibusdam Christianorum domibus
fieri concessum, constitutum et jussum est; unus homo blas-
phemare, reprehendere, conculcare, projicere ac sufflare prae-
sumat.*" . . . Mark the words *unus homo*, hinting at his not
having imitators in his diocese. Claudius himself in his
letters admits that his people were against him, when he
relates their saying to him that they did not believe that
there was any divine thing in the Images, and that they
venerated and honoured them in relation to the originals
represented by them. The fact is, that his subjects were so
badly disposed towards him for his destroying the holy
Figures, that, when he died, the people of Turin were so
furious against him that they gave no rest even to his mortal
remains, and Crosses and holy Images were immediately
restored with applause by the Bishop his successor.

I answer, thirdly, that there are authors in no way favourable to Catholics who confess the historical truth that the

Waldenses were founded by Peter Valdo. It would be too long to quote them all here, but I refer the reader to the "Encyclopedie Metodique-Histoire," tom. 5ᵐᵉ, p. 431, Paris, 1791; the "Cabinet Cyclopedia," History, vol. 11. p. 247, London, 1884; the "English Cyclopedia," by Ch. Knight, Biography, vol. v. p. 479, London, 1857; the "Popular Encyclopedia," vol vi. p. 861, London and Glasgow, 1862. Mr. Schmidt, the author of the "History of the Catharites;" and Mr. Gieseler, of Gottingen, in his letters quoted by Alexis Muston, D.D., in the introduction to his "Israel of the Alps," Glasgow, 1857. The reader will be satisfied if I quote here only four authors. First, Mr. Perrin, amongst a great many mis-statements inserted in his "Histoire des Vaudois," Geneve, 1619, in order to please his Calvinists; (p. 1, ch. ix.) admits that "*Valdo commença a enseigner les peuples les quels de son nome furent appelle Vaudois en l'année de notre Seigneur J. C. Mille cent soixante.*" Second, Alexander Ross, in his "ΠΑΝΣΕΒΕΙΑ," London, 1653, in the catalogue of the twelfth century, says (p. 219), "The Waldenses so called from Waldo of Lyons, who having distributed his wealth professed poverty." Third, Mosheim, "Histoire Ecclesiastique, traduit en François sur la second edition Anglois," Yverdon, 1776, tome III. part ii., ch. v. § xi.; "Origine et Histoire des Vaudois," clearly says, That the sect of the Vaudois is so called from the name of its author Peter, surnamed Waldensis or Valdisius, of Vaux or Valdum, in the Marquisat of Lyons, who employed a Priest to translate the Gospels, &c. into his vernacular language in the year 1160; and that in the year 1180 he stood out as a doctor teaching publicly the doctrine of Christianity in the way in which he understood it," &c. To this passage there is a note saying, "The Vaudois, according to the historians, came from Lyons, and received their name from Peter Waldus, their founder." No one who reads the documents I have here collected concerning the historical Origin of the Waldenses will give any weight to the opposite opinion of the English translator, who in another note, with some unauthorized quotations of Beza, Leger, and others, blames Mosheim for his having written the historical truth against their unfounded assertion. Fourth, Dr. Augustus Neander, in his "General History of the Christian Religion and Church," written in German, and translated by Joseph Terry, London, 1852, vol. viii. pp. 352, 353, writes: " It was quite a mistake to think of deriving this sect (of the Waldenses) from an outward connection with the reforming spirit consequent to the time of Claudius of Turin. . . . All the accounts which go back to the Origin of the sect agree in this, that it started with a rich citizen of Lyons by the name of Peter Waldus (Pierre de Vaux)," &c.

I answer, fourthly and lastly, that the very oldest Waldensian manuscripts, when read in their genuine orig'nals, and when sifted from some unwarranted accounts (which are mere legends), confirm the fact that *Peter Waldensis is the true author of the sect which began and took his name in the latter part of the twelfth century.* Gentle reader, be slow in condemning this my absolute proposition, but read first the following document, which is not published by Morland or by Leger, and in the next chapter my remarks upon the Waldensian documents, particularly " The Noble Leysson," translated and published by them under false dates: and I am convinced that this point of history, called by Bergier (" Dictionnaire de Theologie, Vaudois) *one of the most debated,*" will then be settled indisputably and for ever.

(Waldensian Manuscripts in the library of the University of Cambridge, Vol. A, fols. 36, 37, 38.)

" Now this holy Church, also at the time of the Apostles, grew to many thousands, and in a saintly order, through the vastness of the earth, and remained for a long time in the verdure of holy Religion; and the rulers of the Church perse-

---

" Il n'est peut-être aucune secte dont l'origine ait été plus contestée . . . que la secte Vaudoise.

vered in poverty and humility, according to the old histories,
for about three hundred years, namely, to the time of the
Emperor Constantine Cæsar. But reigning Constantine
leprous there was a ruler in the Church, who was called
Silvester, a Roman. He was living on the Mount Soratte,
near Rome, as we read, on account of the persecution, and
was living the life of a poor man with his own people. As
Constantine received an answer in a dream, as it is related,
he went to Silvester, and was baptized by him in the name
of Jesus Christ, and he was cured from his leprosy.[a] Then,
Constantine, seeing that he, in the name of Jesus Christ,
was cured from so miserable an illness, thought to honour
him who had cleansed him, and left to him the crown and
the dignity of the empire; and Silvester accepted it.[b] But
his companion, as I have it related, parted from him, and
gave not his consent to those things, and kept the way of
poverty.[c] Now Constantine went with a multitude of
Romans into the countries beyond the sea, and then built
Constantinople, as it is called from his name. Then from
that time the heresiarch rose up in honour and dignity, and

Fol. 236. ...

---

[a] The two facts are denied by the most
accurate historians.
[b] This statement is so gross a falsehood
that we are relieved from writing against it;

it was invented for the first time in the
eighth century.
[c] It is not known that the supposed virtuous man ever existed.

E

evils were multiplied upon the earth. We do not believe
after all that the Church of God, on the whole, went out of
the path of truth. But a part failed, and the greater part,
as it commonly happens, was hurled into evil. But the part
which remained, persisted a long time in the truth which
they had received. Thus, by little and little, the sanctity of
the Church failed. Yet, about eight hundred years after Constantine,[20] rose one, whose proper name was Peter, as I have
heard, and he was of a country called Vaudia. He, however, was rich and wise and very good, as our predecessors
say. Then, either by reading it himself or hearing it from
others, he received the word of the Gospel, and sold the
possessions he had, and distributed them to the poor, and
took the path of poverty, and preached, and gathered disciples. . . . He entered then into the city of Rome,[21] and disputed in the presence of the heresiarch on faith and religion.
There was there at that time a Cardinal of Puglia, who was
his friend, and praised his manner of living and his words,
and loved him. Yet at the end he (Peter de Vaudia)
received the answer at the court, that the Roman Church
could not endure his words, and would not abandon the
path she was engaged with. And thus, the sentence being

*gicram be the me beparthe impgmere be is the be armim bel cot, mas tole parma cogir
e la maiat part, raagram en remmm, rmbuthe en mal. Silas la part germme prome
pre moel bramp en aqueta terem in col lip male corrupe. Shapel la mmrret be la
gicram mmmgae por a par. Silas reagrre 9 crut are be Comenem as trbe an la
propl mm bel mi cre b'lere, ruaymm go aumir, mme el cre bumm regem berta Claubla.
Silas agueet, ruagmm blem li marra brcbra maime, re ch e antd e bem l'armeme.
Dence e ri legnm, e audrem br li marre, ceurop tae p'irellem bel cummgrll, e lemlar a
qurllae remm tae rl male e lae beparrle a li patre e prro la brle br pameva e prvbirbr
e le bierlptra, e letre en la rlgra br Romm e bumputa bremrre (fol. 296) la crelmurbe
be le te e be la critigism. Silas en aqusl tromp ria aqul are rarbrmal be galfte la
cal cre mmie be tul, e lammmm la blm be lml e la morella, e cramme tul. R la grele
ceormp crmpert en la cort que la gicram rememm ame pepe perra la morelia be tul, rd

* The Emperor Constantine the Great
died the year of our Lord 337, which added
to 800, makes 1137, the approximative time
of the birth or youth of Peter Waldensis or
the Vaudia, perfectly in accordance with the
author gives above.
* All this part, of Peter Waldensis having

born in Rome, and found a Cardinal friend,
and disputed there personally, is not confirmed by the contemporaries. Some Waldenses went to Rome to obtain the Pope's
sanction in the year 1179 as we have mentioned, Sect. XI.

given, he was cast out of the Synagogue. Nevertheless, he himself preaching in the town made many disciples; and going through the Italian provinces, gathered a multitude of people, so that, in different places, many adhered to their conversation—I mean of him and his successors. And they greatly multiplied, because the people heard them willingly, on account of the word of truth being in their mouths, and of their pointing out the path of salvation. And they so multiplied that there were joined to their teaching sometimes eight hundred, sometimes a thousand, sometimes very few. God worked wonders through them, as we are told by many who readily speak the truth. However, these fruitful works lasted for the space of two hundred years," as we are assured by the elders. At last the envy of Satan and the malignity of wicked men rising up, not a little persecution took place amongst the servants of God, and they were chased from one country to another; and their cruelty against us endures to the present hour." *

---

tun tmio fnbenpgmaa in tai atomtmia. Epma e at aranngia to faye fara ia niaa.
gagu. Rrnd be mena rt mreuryans prtmionut ru in cigen fny pinanta beriginn. C
farren cumin per lan regiona bo Pratia tr atantnmant ratyni gut ra planara perr
anbtrtrm panri en in lar renneramnion, tant rt anrtrpnn tmm fi anrrabm br tni. r
fentn fnamrnt anadtigtica ; ent in pobir amnin ter tmtentier, ranprron ent to gnrafin br
tertin tonm ru in bnrm br int, e trmanrttmm bit br aetn. G analnpltqnrten raar
qnr avtmnrbtrmnani anigttnnm en it tar renarth airnnn ter, a trm, airnnn ter mnti,
atnnn ter n nt put. Din abartn nnrtntitlnn prt ter, raqrnn mn nara br planmn
Scd parinn balnnric trtrin. Attan aqnintnn abtnn fnqtmninn tntrtnn prt tranani
br bni trnt pn, ranprnn rn brnmmntrn ger fi trtij. G fa grrfin, trtnnt nr tranbtrin
ter! anrnant e in mningnren br fi frtien, prntqnntrinn nnn prta tn tn rntrt ti antf br
Dia, e tn gtrrnn int br rngian rn rnginn; e ia rntrtitrn br ter prtnrntn rnrrn nrn
rnmrn nnn.

" If this 200 is added to the 1157 we have the year 1357 pointed out by the writer of the present passage. Consequently this piece was written after the year 1557, and perhaps much later. Mr. Henry Bradshaw

says that the manuscript was written at the beginning of the fifteenth century, at the earliest. (Antiq. Soc., March 16, p. 212, Cambridge, 1862.)

** See the Article XIII. towards the end.

Section XV.

THE DATES WHICH LEGER AND MORLAND HAVE ASSIGNED TO THE WALDENSIAN MANUSCRIPTS ARE COUNTERFEIT.

AGAINST the proofs already quoted for the fact that the Waldensian sect did not exist before the time of Peter of Valdum, and that he is its real father and founder, there might be produced the dates assigned by Morland and Leger to the most ancient Waldensian manuscripts; which dates, if correct, would prove that the sect existed before the time of the said reformer. And in truth John Leger has printed the following dates, fixing

La Nobla Leyçon	At the year A.D.		1100	Page	25
The Catechism	„ „	„	1100	„	38
The Antichrist	„ „	„	1120	„	71
The Purgatory	„ „	„	1126	„	83
The Invocation of Saints	„ „	„	1120	„	87

And, in his Chapter xviii. the first
• Waldensian Confession at the year 1120.

Now, if we clearly prove that the recited dates of Leger have not any ground of truth, and indeed are against the best evidence derived from the same manuscripts, which themselves tell the tale that they were written some centuries after the existence of Peter Waldensis, the last stronghold in support of the fabulous antiquity of the Waldensian sect will be destroyed; and at the same time the impudence of John Leger will be manifested, who so shamefully imposed upon the public, and misled nearly all who wrote on the subject after him. I have said, the impudence of John Leger, because my opinion is that Sir Samuel Morland was also misled by the same Leger, both in what concerns the history of the Waldensian troubles in Piemont, and in what relates to the dates of their manuscripts, given by the same

Leger to Morland, and by Morland deposited in the Cambridge Library, and partly published by him, with an English translation, in his "History of the Evangelical Churches," &c., some twenty-two years before the time in which Leger published, in French, his work bearing the same title, which may be called an enlarged second edition of Morland's. I am persuaded of this, because I cannot be induced to believe that Samuel Morland, an English public man, would wilfully deceive his readers with false and unwarranted statements, had he not been led by Leger to think that they were undeniable facts. And what I have said of Morland, I say also of those many fair and learned English writers, who, not having the means which, after the new discoveries, we now have to sift the wheat from the chaff, have been induced, through the same false statement of Leger, to copy and repeat his assertion again and again. About the public character of John Leger, I shall produce in the next part some historical facts which will show that this my opinion of him is too well grounded.

After this short digression, let us see the true dates of the Waldensian manuscripts, principally of those in the Cambridge Library, because they are the oldest of all, and because they are solely quoted by Morland and Leger. On this argument I follow Professor J. H. Todd ("The Waldensian Manuscripts," Dublin, 1865) and Mr. H. Bradshaw ("Recovery of the Long-lost Waldensian Manuscripts," Antiquarian Society, May 10, 1862, Cambridge), two authors of unexceptionable authority on the matter. "Besides the Dublin collection" (H. Bradshaw, p. 217), "all of which seem to have been written in the sixteenth century (from 1520 to 1530), we have two miscellaneous volumes at Geneva and four at Cambridge—A, B, C, D, as well as more than one copy of the New Testament, all assignable to the fifteenth century; and in addition to these, at Cambridge and at Grenoble, one incomplete and one complete copy of the New Testament, which may be ascribed to the close of the four-

teenth century." With regard to the volume existing at
Geneva, Mr. Bradshaw observes (L. c. p. 204) that it was
"attributed by the librarian there to the twelfth century;
but from the writing of Dr. Todd and other judges, it is
assigned, without hesitation, to the middle or latter half of
the fifteenth."

Let us see now more particularly the dates of the Cambridge manuscripts, in accordance with the order of age,
under the guidance of the same Mr. Bradshaw (L. c. p. 206,
et seq.). Volume F, containing the greater part of the
New Testament and certain chapters of Proverbs and
Wisdom, is assigned to probably the first half of the fifteenth
century. Volume B, containing a good many various pieces,
and " La Nobla Leyçon," with its date partly scratched out,
is assigned to probably the same first half of the fifteenth
century. Volume C, containing some sermons and translations from the Vulgate, and in addition, the beginning of
another copy of " La Nobla Leyçon," with its date in full,
is assigned to the middle of the fifteenth century. Volume
A, containing translations, sermons, instructions and the
historical passage partly stated in our last preceding article,
is assigned to the latter half of the fifteenth century. Volume
D containing sermons, discourses and instructions, is also
assigned to the latter half of the fifteenth century. In
volume E there are different pieces in Latin, and some
moral metrical compositions, and in one place there is
marked the year of O. L. 1521, and in another, 1519. The
handwriting is perfectly in accordance with the sixteenth
century. About the date given by Leger to the first Waldensian Confession of Faith, we shall have a better opportunity of speaking in our Third Part. Besides the criticism
of antiquaries on the style, language and handwriting, by
which the true dates of the manuscripts, as here stated, are
fixed against those imagined by Leger, we may here touch
upon some other internal evidence. First, In the treatise
of the " Invocation of Saints," there is quoted the " Millelo-

quium," which is not of St. Agostin, but of Fra Bartholo-
mews of Urbino, and was written about the middle of the
fourteenth century; and Leger assigned to it the beginning
of the twelfth.   Second, The Catechism contains quotations
from the Bible as divided into chapters; and it is commonly
admitted that the division of the Bible into chapters was
introduced more than two centuries after the date assigned
to it by Leger.   For these first observations I am indebted
to the Rev. P. Allix, D.D. ("Some Remarks," &c., London,
1690), who, having given the above reported reasons, concludes thus (p. 169): "So that it seems these gentlemen
(Morland and Leger) founded their judgments of the
antiquity of these pieces on too weak grounds."   Third, In
the volume A, there is mentioned Doctor Evangelicus, the
title given to the English John Wickliff, who flourished in
the fifteenth century.   And in the same volume there is
also mentioned Peter de Vaudis, who appeared (as it
is there said) about eight hundred years after the Great
Constantine; and facts also are hinted which happened
two hundred years after P. Waldensis (see Article XIV.)
Fourth, The sixth verse of "La Nobla Leyçon," published
by Morland and Leger, as saying: "*Ben ha mil e cent ans
compli entierament*"—"There are a thousand and a hundred
years fully completed"—in fact, has an erasure and an
empty space, in the manuscript Volume B, between *e* and *cent*,
and with a magnifying glass Mr. Bradshaw and others saw
there the number 4 in great part cancelled. If, therefore, this
number be inserted in the proper place, the reading will run
thus: "*Ben ha mil e 4 cent ans compli entierament*"—"There
are a thousand and *four* hundred years fully completed."
And in this case the stronghold of the miraculous Waldensian
antiquity is dismantled.   Fifth, If the said reading should
be uncertain, yet the famous verse of "La Nobla Leyçon"
could not give any ground for placing the existence of the
Waldensian sect before the time of its true founder.   And
here praise is due to the Rev. Th. Sims, M.A., who in his

appendices to "Peyran" (London, 1826, p. 147), speaking
of the supposed 1100 years found in "La Nobla Leyçon,"
according to the printing of Morland and Leger, very wisely
observes that, even on the supposition that 1100 be the true
reading of the manuscript, it cannot be taken as the real
date of the composition. This date, he ingeniously says, is
the time in which the words "*ara sen al derier temps*"—
"now we are at the last time"—were uttered. And this is
plain, if the whole sentence is joined together: "*Ben ha
mil e cent ans: compli entierament que fu scrita lora: ara sen al
derier temps*"—"There are eleven hundred years fully completed since the hour was written: now we are at the last
time." The meaning, then, of the composition is this: that
eleven hundred years are fully passed away from the time
in which the sentence was written: "Now we are at the
last time." Let us ask, then, at what time the words
alluded to were written? The answer is: that the words
"We are at the last time," or "the last hour come,"—
"*Ultima hora venit*"—were written by St. John in his 1st
Ep. chap. ii. v. 18. St. John wrote the said Epistle in his
old age, and at least about seventy years after our Lord's
birth. In consequence, these seventy years are to be added
to the supposed eleven hundred years written in the composition, which will give the real date of the manuscript,
namely, the year eleven hundred and seventy: which shows
that the composition was not written before the time of
Peter de Vaudis. I have endeavoured to place Rev. Th.
Sims' reasoning in the clearest possible light, because it
gives him credit for his ingenious explanation.* Yet we

---

* Antony Monastier, in his seventh chapter, "Origin of the name Vaudois," in order
to maintain that the Waldenses existed before Peter Valdo, amongst other gratuitous
suppositions, after having quoted the name
of *Vallenses*, given to them by Eberard of
Betham, and that of *Waldenses*, given to
them by Abbot Bernard of Fontcauld (*Fontis
calidi*, from whose work I have quoted in
Section IV.), assures his readers that Abbot
Bernard dedicated his work to Pope Lucius
the Third, and that that Pope, who condemned the Waldenses, mentioned by the
Abbot as dead (*seloris recordationis*), was
Lucius the Second, who died in the year
1144; and hence concludes that the con-

do not want this interpretation, as it is now well proved
that the number 1100 is not the true reading of the manuscript: there is no doubt now that it is a composition of
the fifteenth century. Sixth, This appears also by the best
possible evidence from the last page of the manuscript,
Vol. C, in which there are the first fourteen lines of
another copy of "La Nobla Leyçon," and the fifth verse
is fully written thus: "*Ben ha mil e cccc ans compli entierament*"—"There are a thousand and four hundred
years completed fully." "There can be no doubt," says
Mr. Bradshaw (L. c. p. 211), "that the Geneve and
Dublin copies are both later than our two; and, however
we may explain the omission from them, it is at least the
evidence of two earlier against two later copies; and this
. . . seems enough to satisfy the most strenuous advocates
of the antiquity of the poem."

After the alleged evidences in confirmation of my present
argument, it would be a waste of time to add any further
words. Let us then repeat with emphasis the fact that
*Peter Waldensis is the true author of the sect which arose
and was called by his name, in the latter part of the twelfth
century.*

The above-mentioned passages of the two copies of " La Nobla Leyçon " are exhibited at the first page of this book, both for the fuller satisfaction of the learned reader and for a visible evidence of what has been said.

ON THE PERSECUTIONS OF THE WALDENSES.

SECTION I.

CHARACTER OF JOHN LEGER.

ET us begin this Second Part by endeavouring to give the real character of John Leger, the famous historian of the Vaudois, in order to put the reader on his guard about his reports. Samuel Guisbernon, a writer much respected for his accuracy, and a contemporary of Leger, in his History (" Histoire Genealogique de la Royal Maison de Savoje, justifié par titres, manuscripts, ancients monuments et autres prouves autentiques." Lyon, 1660), at pp. 1013 and 1014 writes thus : " The minister Leger (John), the nephew of that (Antony) who was condemned to death and retired to Geneve, is a man of malicious and tumultuous spirit, full of spite and rancour. He, through his secret agents in Geneve, Switzerland, France, Holland, England, Germany and the Northern provinces, spread the report that his Royal Highness, the Sovereign of Piemont, attempted to destroy their Jerusalem (he calls thus the valleys of Lucerna, Angrogna, &c.). He exaggerated the origin of those poor despised descendants from the Vaudois, or Poor of Lyons, . . . and endeavoured to engage in their behalf all the new religions

in any way connected with them. He forged tales of
cruelties so unheard of and extraordinary, that they would
hardly be perpetrated by barbarians; asserting that it is as
true as the Gospel, that they have been practised in their
valleys by the soldiers of H.R.H. to such an extremity,
that by order of the Marquis de Pianezza, the executioner
cut so many throats that the blood of the murdered people
ran through the streets of La Torre. . . . While the truth is
this, that, during the war, two persons only were executed
by the sentence of Senator Parrachin. This trumpet of
sedition published besides, that new kinds of torments were
then invented; that little infants were devoured, and the
brains of the murdered eaten, that the persecution of Dio-
cletianus against the Christians was milder than that practised against the inhabitants of the valleys. And though the
author of all these calumnies had a very bad repute amongst
his own people, yet they created so strong an impression
upon the spirits of the people abroad, that a great sympathy
towards the inhabitants of the valleys was excited, and a
great indignation against the Sovereign of Piemont roused.
Collections were made in their behalf: and in England alone
more than a million of francs* were gathered; out of which
the Minister Leger and his agents received the principal
benefit; from whence a dissension afterwards grew amongst
them. Thence it followed that Cromwell sent Morland to
the Sovereign of Piemont," &c.

Let us see now what is said about John Leger, by the
author of the manuscript ("Histoire veritable"). He thus
speaks of him (p. 762): "John Leger has filled his large
volume with calumnies and falsehoods and fables cunningly
invented. There is no doubt that his uncle Antony was
condemned to death for his crime of rebellion, as it is said
in the sentence which I have read. Whilst the Governor-

---

* Samuel Morland (Thurloe State Papers,
vol. iv. p. 360, London, 1743) speaks of
seven thousand pounds given in England on
that occasion for the Waldenses; and in
another letter he mentions £500 more.

general of H. R. H. was the chief Magistrate of the valleys, and the Counts also represented there the Sovereign, Antony Leger, by his own authority, made himself the master and supreme ruler over all the people, and kept the valleys in an open rebellion against the orders of Amadeus I. and of Mary Christina the Regent in the year 1637. (Pp. 783, 784, 785.) And yet John Leger at page 70 of his volume assures his readers, with impudence, that his uncle Antony was condemned to death after his having been faithful to his Prince in the time of revolution."

"The Regent Mary Christina on the 16 April 1642 issued this order: ' That when any inhabitant of the valleys should become a Catholic, the royal treasurers and receivers of the revenues should pay to the Waldensian commons all the same sums which the convert was used to pay to them.' "

The following are the very words of the order (p. 815):* " In order that this conversion may remain within the limits of a mere and simple favour, so that nobody be damaged, .we command that the treasurers and the revenue officers who are now and shall be for the time being, and that all others to whom shall befit, should accept and make a return of money to the tax gatherers of the (Waldensian) communities, to the amount of all the impositions and charges due by each one of the converts, as if they by themselves should pay the amount in cash."

Now John Leger has printed (L. c.) the falsehood that Christina obliged the Waldenses, who remained heretics, to pay to her treasures all the charges from which the new converts to Catholicity were exonerated. Which falsehood

---

* *Affinchè questa conversione venti ne' suoi termini di pura e mera grazia, di modo che nessuno ne senta pregiudizio; ordiniamo che i tesorieri e ricevitori presenti e d'avvenire, e a chi sarà espediente, di accettare e rimettere agli esattori delle comunità, come se le pagassero in contanti, le somme a che ascenderanno gl'imposti e cariche suddetti di cadauno di essi (convertiti).*

was also printed before by Morland (p. 274); in accordance
(I believe) with the deceitful instructions of the same Leger,
or of his uncle Antony; in these words: "Although the
mystery of all this is . . . that those burdens which are
taken off the shoulders of the revolters, should be laid
upon the backs of those who persevere in the true religion,
the better to break and destroy them."

The reader will remember all the misstatements of J.
Leger, which have been pointed out in the first part, in
relation to the authorities of Reinerius Sacco, Pilichdorff,
Champion, Arch. Seyssell, Rorengo, Belvedere, &c., distorted
by him, and made to say the very contrary to their plain
and natural meaning; and also his having given false dates
to the old Waldensian manuscripts, &c.; and judge that it
is right to apply to him that saying of Luther, reported by
Rorengo ("Esame," &c. p. 37): "*Qui semel mentitur ex
Deo non est, et in omnibus suspectus habetur.*"

I will conclude this paragraph with another very striking
document bearing on John Leger's character. Amongst the
Miscellanea Patria of the King's library of Turin I have
read a darkened printed paper of the year 1662, of which I
here subjoin the extract, and a literal translation of the
principal part. "The delegates of H. R. H. in criminal
causes in the valleys of Lucerna, St. Martino and Perosa,
against John Leger, Minister, born in the Valley of St.
Martino, declare: That the third summons has been sent to
the Minister John Legero to appear, in order to make his
defence in relation to the many atrocious crimes, not concerning Religious matters, but of high treason against men,
imputed to him. Namely, for many murders committed by
his order or with his consent; comprising the murder of
his servant, to conceal his having got her with child, and so
not to lose his ministry; and for his having enrolled, and
paid with money usurped from the commons, brigands,
authors of misdeeds both against those of his own religion
and creed, and against the representatives of the King, &c.,

&c. "That, as he did not appear under the security offered to him, to make his defence, a trial has been instituted, and he has been judged guilty of high treason against men for crimes committed by him from the beginning of the year sixteen hundred and fifty-six and since; crimes which do not relate to matters of Religion: and being guilty, he deserves to be condemned, as now he is condemned to be exiled for ever, and to have his goods confiscated; and if he should come into the hands of justice, to be publicly hung till his soul be separated from his body: then his body to be left hanging by one foot for twenty-four hours; after which it is ordered that his head be separated from his body, and exposed in the square of St. John, in the valley of Lucerna, upon the infamous column." The sentence was confirmed by the Senate with the following words:[*] "By public decree of this Senate to be engraved on stone tables, we determine that the sentence now recited, and justly pronounced against the abominable John Logero, guilty of high treason of the first order relating men, be put into execution. The year sixteen hundred and sixty-two."

This will be enough for the present to show what reliance is to be placed on the assertions of the celebrated historian of the Waldensian churches of Piemont.

SECTION II.

THE CONDUCT OF THE WALDENSES IN PIEMONT.

HE true history of the conduct of the Waldenses in Piemont will show that the reason of their having been often punished was not precisely their religion; it was their breaking the laws of the country.

---

[*] *Sententiam nunc recitatam et in refundum Joannem Logerum, tanquam Lesæ Majestatis humanæ in primo capite reum, justa prolatam, executioni demandandam esse, publico Senatus Consulto lapideis tabulis consignando, determinus,* 1662.

We repeatedly read of the poor Waldenses being persecuted as well by the rigorous Inquisition, between the years 1206 and 1228, as by the Piemontese Sovereigns; as, for example, in 1400, when, in the depth of winter, they were forced to fly to the mountains, and four score of them were frozen to death; and also by the sentence of the justices condemning them to be burnt to death, as was particularly done in December 1475 in Susa, and in Turin, &c. Without denying similar facts, which, however, have been often much exaggerated, I think we may trace the reason of this hard treatment by examining old documents. I begin with a letter of Pope Innocent VIII. dated May 1487, and printed by Morland himself (p. 199): by which the Pontiff authorized the Archdeacon of Cremona, Albert de Capitaneis, to proceed against the heretics, and to invoke also, if necessary, the assistance of the armed hands of the civil power. "The heretics," the Pope says,* "have endeavoured to draw the faithful into their errors, have despised the censures of the Church, robbed the goods, and destroyed the house of the Inquisitor, killed his servant, made war against their temporal Masters, and committed a great many other like abominations." No wonder, then, if the Waldenses, being so guilty, were punished with such exemplary rigour.

I continue with the MS. of Vegezzi, founded upon the Piemontese annals: "In the year 1535, Francis I. King of France, occupied with his army the state of Piemont. The Waldenses, on this occasion, springing out of the limits prescribed to them, sword in hand, invaded the neighbouring places, pillaging the castles and wounding the people of the feudatories. At this time Francis was using all means to destroy the Huguenots in his kingdom; and he issued an

---

* *Alios Christi fideles in eosdem errores protrahere, Censuras vilipendere, domum habitationis ejusdem (Inquisitoris) subvertere, et quæ in eo erant bona diripere et derubare; ejusdem Inquisitoris famulum interficere; contra eum hostili modo inire, illorum Dominis temporalibus resistere, . . . infinita quoque alia detestabilia ac abhorrenda facinora perpetrare scriti non fuerint.*

order that the Parliament of Turin should also persecute
the Waldenses. And on this occasion more than one of
them was burnt, according to the barbarous laws of the
time, in the public squares. After the death of King
Francis and the peace of Cambresis (3 April 1559), Em-
manuel Filibertus was restored to his states. He intended
to clear his dominion from the heretics, and expelled the
Waldenses from the places occupied by them out of their
limits: and perhaps he might have cast them out of the
valleys altogether, had they not been strengthened by a
body of French sectarians. Though now left unmolested
the Waldenses rose again after a short time, and, guided by
their heretic minister, and helped by four hundred armed
Frenchmen, fought against the castles of Filibertus. After
many battles, the Count of Trinity conquered them. And
also on this occasion many executions took place."

Now we shall read the author of the "Veritable Histoire"
(p. 614): "About 1375 the Waldenses again offended against
the laws of their Sovereign. The Parish Priest of La Torre,
named Braide, was murdered by them in his own house.
They had already denied him the necessaries of life in order
to compel him to go away, which he, faithful to his obliga-
tions, had refused to do." (P. 615.) "The Parish Priest of
Dublon, who, by his good example and zeal, intended to
keep his Catholic flock in their faith, was also murdered by
them while exercising his pastoral duties in a poor house.
The same Waldenses plotted to kill other zealous Priests
attending to the spiritual welfare of their Catholics. A
layman, named Vincent Buriasco, a fervent Catholic, who
was with the Priests, informed them of the plot in good
time, and the Priests were saved. The sectarians, finding
that their project was baffled through him, took their vengeance and killed poor Buriasco instead. The heretics,
being unsuccessful in their design of killing Andrew Tos-
cani, a notary who lodged the Duke's soldiers in his own
house, after the departure of the soldiers, entered into his

F

house, plundered it, and killed the women found there. As it was then time of war, no punishment was inflicted on the murderers, and, in consequence, they grew every day more and more daring in their misdeeds. They robbed the altars, burnt on them the most Holy Sacrament and the images of the Saints, and (except in Lucerna) hindered the performance and celebration of the Holy Mysteries throughout the valleys in which they were simply tolerated." (P. 617.) "All these bad actions, and a great many more crimes, too long to be enumerated, had been perpetrated by the Waldenses during the space of thirty years, till 1600, without being duly punished, on account of the continual wars of the time. We can state with certainty that, in the said period, through the treachery and restless violence of the heretic ministers, and of their Waldenses, who already had become Calvinists, several hundred persons perished in the valleys by violent deaths." (P. 618.) "After this, it cannot be surprising if an order was published by the Duke obliging the Protestants to retire within five days into the limits already assigned to them, or to abjure their errors in case that they chose to remain out of their limits amongst Catholics." (Pp. 619, 620.) "As the order was not obeyed in any way, and the Calvinist ministers continued their persecutions against the Catholic Priests who were sent to them, the Duke then issued another order, not unjust, but yet more rigorous and more strictly binding." (P. 755.) "Victorius Amedeus I. died of a violent illness, and Princess Mary Christina, his wife, obtained the Regency of the State. She published a new decree (the 19th October 1637) against the ever-disobedient Waldenses, requiring them to retire within their limits in the valleys, according to decrees already published: the order to be executed within three days' time, under the threatened penalties. The 9th of November following, the order was renewed. Nevertheless, the people of the valleys continued in their disobedience, nay, sword in hand, stood against the Princess. Antony Leger, the uncle of John Leger, the false historian of the valleys, was their leader."

(P. 797.) "It is to be remarked that there were, from the ancient times, Catholic Churches in the valleys, and John Leger himself allows it in some parts of his volume, though in other places he denies it, in accordance with his fashion of contradicting himself. In our time also (*at the latter part of the seventeenth century*) the miserable ruins of those old buildings may be seen. They were consecrated to our Lord with the names of the Saints, after whom they were named, as to our powerful intercessors with God and with His only Mediator Jesus Christ. It is also to be remarked that the sectarians demolished them, for the most part, after the year 1550, as up to that time the said Churches were still standing. And this act of impiety was executed with the help of foreign armies in time of war, when parish Priests, Priors, Religious men, and Clergy were cast out of them. Besides, it is not to be forgotten that the Waldenses, in order to obtain pardon for having so destroyed the Churches, entered into an obligation with their Sovereign to rebuild them at their own expense."

I conclude this section by observing that more than once the Waldenses confessed that they had been guilty of grievous crimes. Among the documents, by which this observation may be proved, I choose the following petition, signed by twenty-four Waldensian deputies, with the rescript of their Prince.

(P. 516.)* "Our most Serene Lord and Prince. Your poor and most humble subjects of the Valleys della Perosa, Lucerna, Angrogna, Roccapiatta, San Bartolomeo, and Prà Rustino, approach with very deep respect to humble ourselves at the feet of your most Serene Highness, and to beg

---

* *Serenissimo Signore e Principe Nostro.*
Li suoi poveri ed umilissimi sudditi della valli della Perosa, Lucerna, Angrogna, Roccapiatta, San Bartolomeo e Prà Rustino, vengono con ogni riverenza ad umiliarsi ai piedi di V. A. Serenissima tutti a chiederli perdono

pardon with halters on our necks, supplicating that you be pleased to show your usual benignity and mercy towards us, and that you would not keep before your eyes our great faults and our great misdeeds, because *we have not kept that loyalty which was due to you from us*, who are your most humble subjects and servants," &c.

(P. 538.) The rescript, dated 21st November 1594, contains the following expressions:

* " Both for having taken arms against His Highness, and for having caused many damages, many destructions, and conflagrations, both in particular and in general, both against His Highness and against His Ministers and other particular persons of the State," &c.

Section III.

SKETCH OF EVENTS CONNECTED WITH THE SUPPOSED WALDENSIAN MASSACRE OF 1655.

BEFORE entering into the particular accounts relating the catalogue of the supposed barbarous murders described by John Leger, I think it advisable to recall to the reader's mind the substance of the general facts connected with the said particular details. Finding these facts faithfully reported by Lingard ("History of England," vol. xi. chap. i.), I will endeavour to give here his narrative, as shortly as possible, in his own words.

" The Duke of Savoy often confirmed to the native Wal-

col laccio al collo; supplicandola di volere usare della solita benignità e clemenza sua verso noi, e non riguardare ai gran falli e mancamenti nostri in non avere conservata quella fedeltà che gli dovevamo, come umilissimi sudditi e servitori suoi, etc. etc.

* *Sì per aver tolto le armi contro sua Altezza, quanto per aver commessi molti danni, molte ruine e incendii sì in particolare quanto in generale, e tanto contro Sua Altezza quanto suoi Signori Ministri e altri particolari dello Stato. 21 Novembre, 1594.*

denses the free exercise of their Religion, on condition that
they should confine themselves within their ancient limits.
Complaints were made that several of them had formed
settlements and established their worship without their
borders. The Court of Turin referred the decision of the
dispute to the civilian Andrea Gastaldo. After a long and
patient hearing, he pronounced a definitive judgment, that
Lucerna and some other places lay without the original
boundaries, and that the intruders should withdraw, under
the penalties of forfeiture and death. Permission, however,
was given to them to sell for their own profit the lands
which they had planted. At first they submitted sullenly
and sent deputies to Turin to remonstrate. But a few days
afterwards a fast was proclaimed; their ministers excommunicated every individual who should sell his lands in the
disputed territory. The natives of the French valleys
united with the natives of those belonging to the Duke of
Savoy, bound themselves by an oath to stand by each other
in their common defence: and messages were despatched to
solicit aid from Geneva and the other Protestant cantons of
Switzerland. The Marquis Pianezza, the chief minister of
the Duke, alarmed by the intelligence, marched from Turin
with an armed force to suppress the nascent confederacy:
reduced La Torre, where the insurgents had a garrison of
six hundred men, offered pardon to all who should submit,
and fixed his quarters in Bobbio, Villar, and lower Angrogna. The insurgents promised that the soldiers should
be peaceably received. But the Duke's soldiers found the
bare walls, the inhabitants having already retired to the
mountains with their cattle and provisions. Quarrels ensued
between the parties, and the desire of vengeance provoked a
war of extermination. But the military were in general
successful.

"Accounts teeming with exaggerations and improbabilities
were transmitted to the different Protestant states. The
Duke of Savoy was represented as a bigoted and intolerant

prince, the Vaudois as an innocent race, whose only crime
was their attachment to the reformed faith. The Protestant
powers were implored to assume their defence; pecuniary
contributions were called for to save from destruction by
famine the remnant which had escaped the edge of the
sword. In England the cause was advocated in print and
from the pulpit; a solemn fast was kept, and the passions of
the people were roused to enthusiasm. The ministers in a
body waited on Cromwell to recommend the Vaudois to his
protection. And he first, through Stouppe, the minister of
the French Church in London, offered them his support,
and to transplant them to Ireland." The first was accepted,
the other declined. Next, he solicited the King of France
to join with him in mediating for them, and received in
answer that Louis had already interposed his good offices,
and expected a favourable result: and, lastly, he sent Morland as ambassador to Turin, where he was honourably received and entertained at the Duke's expense. It was in
August in the year 1655 when Morland was authorized to
announce that the Duke, at the request of the King of France,
had granted an amnesty to the Vaudois, and confirmed their
ancient privileges; that the boon had been gratefully received by the insurgents; and the natives of the valleys,
Protestant and Catholic, had met, embraced each other with
tears, and sworn to live in perpetual amity together."

I conclude this true sketch of facts related by Lingard, by
transcribing a document from the papers of Thurloe, the secretary of Cromwell, given by the same author in a foot-note.
It relates to the supposition that a regiment of Irish Papists,
commanded by Prince Thomas of Savoy, was with Pianezza:
and to them were attributed, of course, the most horrible

" Amongst the State Papers of Thurloe
quoted above, there are (vol. iii. pp. 458–461)
extracts of letters written to Stouppe by
Mr. Leger (Antony, the uncle of John, are
the first section of this part): in which the
fact is confirmed that his highness, the Lord
Protector, had really offered to give in Ireland some lands to the poor exiled; and that
the Waldensian Ministers did not accept the
offering on the ground that they could not
forsake their churches, which can prove
their succession from the time of the Apostles,
&c. We have shown the falsehood of this
last assertion in the first part.

barbarities. On inquiry, it was discovered that these supposed Irishmen were English (Thurloe, paper iii. 50) : "The Irish regiment, said to be there, was the Earl of Bristol's regiment, a small and weak one, most of them being English. I hear not such complaints of them as you set forth."

Section IV.

THE PARTICULAR MURDERS OF THE YEAR 1655 DESCRIBED BY LEGER, CONFRONTED WITH THE LEGAL STATEMENTS OF THE SAME FACTS.

IN accordance with the statement of the often-quoted manuscript, "Histoire Veritable des Vaudois," I will now relate the true details of the supposed cruel Waldensian massacre of the year 1655, described by John Leger (liv. II. chap. ix.), and shamefully misrepresented by him, with indecent engraved figures: the very identical engravings and descriptions published more than twenty years before in Morland's history, which, as we have before said, there is every reason to think, is almost entirely an inspiration of the same Leger, and may be reckoned to be his first edition.

Leger says, first (L. C.), that "the particulars of the massacre have been confirmed through the evidence of more than 150 persons of irreproachable honesty and credibility, who made their depositions at the office of two notaries, Bianchi and Mondonis." (MS. pp. 162-164.) "We may forgive John Leger for not mentioning the names of these 150 respectable persons; it would have made his volume too thick. Nevertheless, we are entitled to know that their evidences were given at the office of persons to be trusted. Unhappily for Leger, this is not the case. The notary Bianchi was his right hand in every bad enterprise, and a criminal on account of his misdeeds, and therefore condemned to death by public sentence the 23rd May, 1655. Mondone was not a notary in the year 1655, when it is supposed that the depositions were made. Mondone obtained the office of notary four years afterwards, in 1659; and, besides, in 1663 and 1664, he declared that he had received no depositions of the kind. This fact of the two notaries of Leger is enough by itself to prove in general that the massacres detailed by him are not authentic." (*See* Art. 1. of this part.)

As Leger says that he gave the original of the depositions, signed by the notaries Bianchi and Mondone, to Samuel Morland, the Commissary of Cromwell in Italy, and that he (Leger) published the same depositions, translated from an Italian copy kept by himself;* the intelligent reader will understand that the narrative of these facts, published by Morland more than twenty years previously to the publication of Leger's, is really the fictitious narrative of Leger himself; and that the manuscript of the depositions, placed by Sir Samuel Morland in the Cambridge Library, is the original manuscript of the fictitious narrative given by Leger to Morland.

We will now examine the particular stories. To avoid confusion, the matter will be divided into two columns. That at the left of the reader containing the assertions of Leger, that at the right giving the true statement of the facts which Leger has distorted.

---

* (*Histoire*, Part II. pp. 116, 117.) " J'en ay remis l'original signé des Notaires Bianchi et Mondonis entre les mains de Monsieur Morland, commissaire extraordinaire du Mon Lord Protecteur de la Grande Bretagne, comme il le confesse au 6 Chapitre du second livre de son histoire ; ma contralant d'en avoir conservé la fidèle copie. Voici donc le contenu des susdites depositions fidèlement traduit de l'Italien."

John Leger's Assertions and Representations.	The true legal Statements.

John Leger's Assertions and Representations.

Sara Rostagnol is described as tormented, having her belly cut open, because she refused to invoke the Virgin Mary; at last beheaded by a soldier.

The true legal Statements.

(MS. p. 1065.)

Sara Rostagnol was stabbed twice and wounded grievously in the head, while she was handing weapons to the rebels. No other injury. And she died afterwards in a place called La Maddalena delle Vigne, as is deposed by six persons of her own religion :—

David Alliota, David Grainer, James Chiaror, Joseph Crespin, Daniel Pavarin, James Berger, the 16th February, 18th and 19th March, 1674, at the office of Dondino, a notary of known respectability, and esteemed also by the Vaudois.

Martha Costantina, wife of James Barrel, had her belly ripped open; her private parts and breasts cut out, which the Duke's soldiers cooked, made a stew of them, and then eat them.

Martha Costantina, wife of Barrel, died before the year 1655, as is proved at the office of Bandino by six of her own religion :
David Alliota, David Grainer, John Roavel, John H. Allian, Antony Presciut, Daniel Massan, the 15th February, and 3rd, 6th, 28th March, 1674.

James Micholin, of Bobbio, a Gentleman, stabbed in his feet, hand, and ears; his private parts cut off, and a lighted candle put to the wound; the nails extracted with pincers, and his head bound with cords so tightly as to force his eyes out of their sockets, and his brains out of his head: and all these torments were inflicted on him in order to oblige him to abjure his religion.

(MS. p. 1066.)

James Michelin, of Bobbio, a Valet, not a Gentleman, born in Frassinier, was simply wounded in one of the combats of 1655, and then carried to Dauphiny : he seven years afterwards was seen in good health in the valley of Locarno, as is confirmed at the office of Bandino, the 23rd December, 1673, by John Michelin, a Vaudois of Bobbio, having his dwelling-house at Villar; and also by John Martinat, of Bobbio, a catholic, at the office of Simondetti, a notary, the 10th March the same year.

John Leger's Assertions and Representations.	The true Legal Statements.
An old man precipitated from a very high rock.	(MS. p. 1086.) About the supposed old man so precipitated, as Leger tells us that he himself is the only witness of this incredible fact, there is no need of any proof to contradict it.
Imias Grand of Angrogna, ninety years of age, beheaded, and then cut into pieces; his bowels spread on the streets, and his limbs hung on trees.	(MS. p. 1087.) No man named Imias Grand existed in Angrogna at that time, or long before that time. This is proved by the depositions of Jovenal Jacoma, of La Torre, of John Ytalliot and Antony Preveial, of Angrogna, made on the 1st February, and 3rd and 6th March, 1674, at the Bandino's office: and of Michael Gonin, of St. Giovanni, made on the 28th March, 1674, at the office of Simondetti.
The wife of Daniel Armand also cruelly tormented.	The wife of Daniel Armand was simply killed through a stab, in a place called Cogno, while she was handing arms to the rebels fighting against the Duke's soldiers. Moyse Yisimor, Antony Simond, James Chabriel, and Peter Nicollet, of La Torre, confirmed this fact at the office of Bandino the 1st February and the 5th, 6th March; and the same was done by David Dalmono, of Villar, at the office of Simondetti, the 10th March, 1674. (The names of all the witnesses are always given in the MS., but I intend to omit them on the following depositions, both for brevity and not to weary the reader.)

John Leger's Assertions and Representations.	*The true Legal Statements.*
	(MS. p. 1087.)
Two women, at a place called La Sarzena, had their bellies ripped open, and their bowels thrown out, by Paul de Pencalier, a captain, the 22nd April, 1655.	There are depositions of five witnesses, all Vaudois, made at the Bandino's office, dated the 9th and 20th February, and the 5th and 6th March, 1674, stating that no woman was killed at that time at the Sarzena; and that Captain Paul de Pencalier was not seen in the mentioned place during the whole of the year 1655.
	There is besides one deposition at the same office, dated the 6th March, 1674, saying that some woman fell into a precipice near La Sarzena, and that she was not injured by any body.
	(MS. p. 1088.)
Maria Raymond, the widow of James Coin, was found in a cave, her bones on one side and her flesh picked off on the other side.	Unhappily for the calumniator, Maria Raymond died many years before 1655. Witnesses, three Waldenses and two Catholics. The depositions at the office of Bandino are on the 7th of January, and 2nd, 6th, and 25th March, 1674.

"This wicked author" (says the author of the MS. L. c.)
"thus imposes upon the credulity of the Protestant people ;
and believes that they will be amused with this kind of
execrable stories. He supposes them to be wild beasts, and
black souls longing to be nourished with the poison of
slander."*

---

* " C'est ainsi que cet écrivain scélérat abuse impudemment de la crédulité
des peuples Protestans qu'il croit prendre plaisir à ce sort des fables exécra-
bles ; les prenans pour brutes et pour des âmes noires qui aiment a se nourrir
du venin de la médisance."

John Leger's Assertions and Representations.	The true Legal Statements.
	(MS. p. 1088.)
Magdalen, worn out with age, the widow of Peter Pilon, of Villar, was found cut into pieces in a cave.	About this Magdalen, widow of Peter Pilon, it has been legally proved by seven witnesses, all Waldenses, in the presence of two notaries, Simondetti and Baudino, that *neither such a widow nor such a husband were at any time at Villar.* The depositions bear the dates of 26th December, 1673, 23rd February, and 2nd, 5th, 9th, 10th March, 1674.
	(MS. p. 1089.)
Anna, daughter of John Carbonier, was violated, a pike driven through her private parts, and then impaled, and raised up and carried by the soldiers through the principal streets as a sort of cross-standard, in order to inspire terror into the passengers.	This daughter of Carbonier, naturally crippled and stupid, was simply found dead in a place called La Grand Rak, without any wound or mark of outrage on her body. Thus says the deposition of five Waldenses at the office of Baudino, the 2nd, 5th, 6th, and 9th of March, 1674.

The author of the manuscript here reproaches John Leger for his shameless indecency and scandalous falsehoods.

John Leger's Assertions and Representations.	The true Legal Statements.
	(MS. p. 1092.)
Many little children tormented, lacerated whilst alive, and precipitated from the top of the rocks.	It is proved by five Waldenses and by two Catholics, who made their depositions the 6th and 9th March, 1673, and the 7th February, 1674, that out of the children of John Andrew Michelin, of La Torre, supposed to be so killed, one died in the year 1656, and the other two, a male and a female, were still alive in 1674. The same is confirmed of the other children.

John Leger's Assertions and Representations.	*The true Legal Statement.*
James Prin and John Gonnet were cruelly tormented in different manners, and thus killed.	(MS. p. 1092). Prin and Gonnet were made prisoners of war, and died natural deaths in the prisons of Lucerna without suffering any torment. The evidence at the office of Simondetti and Bandino bears the name of three Waldenses, the 24th February, the 10th and 16th March, 1674. The same is confirmed by the Marquis of Angrogna, who procured for them charitable assistance in the prison.
John Pellanchon tied to the tail of a mule, and dragged along, and indecently and cruelly tormented.	(MS. p. 1093.) About John Pellanchon, at the office of Simondetti, there are the depositions of Prior Valloro and of David Dalmazzo, a Waldensis, who had been present at the fact, and ascertained that it is true that an insolent soldier had really tied the poor Pellanchon to the tail of a mule, intending that he be thus drawn to Lucerna; but Matolin, the Commander of the Duke's soldiers, having caused Pellanchon to be immediately untied, punished the soldier with imprisonment.
Magdalene Fontaine, only ten years old, killed while the brutal soldiers attempted to violate her.	It has been legally proved by the evidence of two Waldenses, the 2nd and 16th March, 1674, that Magdalene Fontaine was still alive in the said year, 1674.
A mother, flying from the pursuers with her baby on her head, left the baby in the snow. Mercier Tolosano saw this. The Duke's soldiers cut the poor baby into four quarters.	Through the deposition of two Waldenses, 20th February, 1674, it is proved that the soldiers had the baby carried to the nearest village, and she was fed and taken care of for many years, till she died by natural illness in the valley of St. Martino.

John Leger's Assertions and Representations.	*The true Legal Statements.*
Another girl, also only ten years old, was impaled with a pike by the soldiers and then roasted and eaten by them.	(MS. p. 1094.) Three Waldenses of Bobbio juridically affirmed, 26th December, 1673, and 20th February and 10th March, 1674, that the said girl, being foolish, concealed herself in a heap of bushes, to which the soldiers, unaware of it, set fire, and thus she was harmt accidentally.
James Michelin, the father of the late Minister of Angrogna, and two countrymen shamefully bound in their private parts, and thus cruelly tormented.	(MS. p. 1095.) James Michelin, the father of the late Minister, did not suffer any bad treatment. He was made a prisoner of war in a combat, and died by natural illness in the prison of Turin. About the two countrymen, there is nobody who saw or heard anything of them. These are the legal depositions of five Waldenses at the two notaries' offices, 30th December, 1673, and 6th, 9th, 10th March, 1674, besides other five depositions made by Catholics of Bobbio and of La Torre.
Jane Rostagnol, eighty years old, murdered by cutting out her nose, ears, and all extremities of her body.	Jane Rostagnol, who was not as old as it is said, simply died by a gun-shot during a combat near the Alp of Crosurm, as was legally stated by four Waldenses and by two Catholics, the 26th December, 1673, and the 10th March, 1674.

John Leger's Assertions and Representations.	*The true Legal Statements.*
Many persons, as Daniel Salvajot, Louis Terro, Bartholemy Durand, were dreadfully killed by having gunpowder put into their ears and mouths, which, on being set fire to, blew out their brains through their split heads.	(MS. p. 1096.) All these are forgeries. Daniel Salvajot was killed by a gun-shot during the war in a place called La Rombe de Pacalas. Louis Turso was also killed by a gun-shot and a stab received in an attack at a place called Cassa de Roras; and the same was the fate of Bartholemy Durand, at Baumes. None died having received any of the forged injuries. Three Waldenses of Lo Vigna, near Roras, affirmed this juridically, the 26th February, and the 18th and 19th March, 1674.
Daniel Revel was barbarously murdered as the above-named.	Daniel Revel was dead long before the year 1655. Daniel Paradiso and James Bergier proved this fact in a legal deposition the same year, 1674.
Paul Roinaud was also killed in the same cruel manner.	Four Waldenses legally proved at the offices of the often-mentioned notaries, the 6th December, 1673, and the 9th and 20th February, 1674, that Paul Roinaud was found dead after a conflagration, probably suffocated by the smoke. His body was found without any injury on his ears or mouth, and only with his beard and shirt a little burnt.
John Rome, a schoolmaster, had his nails pulled out with pincers; hands, feet and ears perforated in many parts; was asked several times	(MS. p. 1097.) All these cruel details of torments are forged by Leger, as is his custom, to make the Invocation of Saints and the Mass odious to the Protestants,

John Leger's Assertions and Representations.	*The true Legal Statements.*
to invoke the Virgin Mary, and to go to Mass, and at each of his refusals, a piece of his flesh was cut off with a knife.	(MS. p. 1097.) and to insert false motives of Religion into the invented cruelties. The fact is simply this, that Rono was made prisoner of war, and ordered to be transported to Lacerna. But he resisted the soldiers with all his might, and one of them shot him dead with a pistol. This has been juridically confirmed by the Prior, Michael Angel Gallina, and by the Signori Benottino and Vocoro, all men of honour, and as such respected by the Waldenses of Lacerna themselves.
Paul Garnier, of Roras, had his eyes forced out of his head, his private parts cut off and put into his mouth; then he was skinned alive, and left so to die; while his skin, cut into pieces, was hung at four windows of the best houses of Lacerna.	There is a juridical statement of eight Waldenses, named in the MS. bearing the dates of 25th, 26th, 28th February, and 6th, 18th, 19th, 28th March, 1674, asserting unanimously that Paul Garnier was killed by a gun-shot while he was assaulting the town of Lacerna with his companions; and that, after the brigands were driven back, Joseph Baptist Bianco, a Catholic, attended to the burial of his body.
Daniel Cardon, of Roccapiatta, was beheaded, his brains thrown out of the skull and eaten by the soldiers, and his heart devoured by them.	(MS. p. 1098.) The only truth about Daniel Cardon, of Roccapiatta, is that the soldiers of the Duke shot him dead whilst he was fighting with rebels against them, near the temple of Roccapiatta. He had no other injury, and was buried by his own people after the combat. This is the legal deposition made by five of his own companions, the 9th and 28th February, and 6th, 10th, 28th March, 1674.

John Leger's Assertions and Representations.

Margaret Revel, called La Cartara, was burnt by the Duke's soldiers at La Vigne, and so they also served Mary Praviglielmo. The wife of Mathew Giordano is quoted as the eye witness of the fact.

The widow of John Hagon, infirm and bedridden for three years, was carried to La Torre on a cart, wounded with the sharp end of halberds, stoned and drowned in the river Angrogna.

P. Gilles, of La Torre, wounded by a gun-shot, had his nose cut off and his face scarified, and left thus to die.

The true Legal Statements.
(MS. p. 1099.)

Margaret Revel was burnt to death, not by the soldiers, but accidentally; not at La Vigne, but at a place called Li Ronchi, near the farm of Antony Prascinio, where she had concealed herself, without it being known by anybody. Mary Praviglielmo died a natural death in a place called Rocca Cordora. The wife of Mathew Giordano, quoted as an eye witness, was dead and buried long before the year 1655. Thus it is stated by three Waldenses in their depositions at the two notaries', 30th December, 1673, and 28th February and 28th March, 1674.

Four Waldenses, the 6th and 10th March, 1674, made their legal statement to this effect: that the widow of John Hagon, who was not, in fact, infirm, was killed through being stabbed twice by the soldiers, while she was helping the rebels during an attack on a place called "La Gran Rua."

(MS. p. 1100.)

It is not stated by Leger whether this P. Gilles was named Peter or Paul. However, the falsehood of the assertion is proved by the legal evidence of three Waldenses, of La Torre, and of others, as it appears from the registers of the 9th, 24th, and 28th February, and 6th and 10th May, 1674. The statements say, that no man named Paul Gilles was ever known at La Torre; and that there have been known two Gilles named Peter: the one died before the year 1655, and the other died some years after the said date.

G

John Leger's Assertions and Representations.	The true Legal Statements. (MS. p. 1100).
At Gracillane, a place at the bottom of the valley of Lucerna, a great many poor Waldenses were violently cast into an oven already made hot, and ready to bake bread. They were all forced into the oven and roasted alive. Some Catholics were witnesses.	The whole of the account about the furnace of Gracillane, both in its substance and in its circumstances, is another solemn falsehood of a man of unblushing effrontery, as is proved at the office of the two notaries, by the deposition of eleven persons of the same place.

"It would be too long and tedious to continue relating all the legal evidences registered against the forged accounts of John Leger. It will be enough to say, that we are ready to show them to any person who should be doubtful of their genuineness.* Yet, before concluding this argument, we shall touch cursorily some of the other facts misrepresented by J. Leger.

"John Baptist André died before the year 1655 (Deposition, Febr. and March the 7th, 1674), and it is said that he was cut in pieces in the said year 1655.

"(MS. p. 1102.) Michael Belia, said to have had his head rooted out from his shoulders in 1655, was still alive in 1656. (Deposition of five Waldenses, Febr. and March, 1674.)

"Daniel Pellenc, said to have been ignominiously carried to Angrogna by the Catholics; he was really so carried, not by the Catholic soldiers, but by his own Waldenses, in order to get his money. (Deposition, Febr. and March, 1674, ten witnesses.)

"About Michael Perisa, said to have been beheaded at Cavour the same year, 1655, it is proved that there were two men of this name, one died before the said year, the other was still alive in 1674. (Depos. 1674.)

"John Donna, Leger said to have been burnt alive. Seven

---

* (MS. p. 1101.) "Je ne laisse pas de conserver les pièces originales qui justifiant incontestablement le saccard des massacres particuliers, qu'il décrit si au long dans ses rôlles. Elles satisferont ceux a qui il prendroit envie de s'en éclarcir.

witnesses stated legally that there were three persons of this name. The first, wounded in a combat at San John, died of the wound at Angrogna. The second died in 1661, after having been stabbed twice in his belly by another Waldensis, and the third died in 1663 in the mountain of Rubbian.

"It is said that the wife of Paul Chevet was beheaded in the year 1655, and it is proved that she was dead some years previous to that time. (Depos. 1674, four witnesses.)

"Joseph Claret, who while with the brigands trying to take Lucerna by assault, died of a gun-shot, without suffering any other injury, as is confirmed by eight witnesses; is yet described by Leger as having his belly ripped open, in order to take off his fat before his death.

"Mary Paul also, it is said, was killed the same year, 1655; and Mathew Thurin is described as dreadfully tormented, and his body given to the dogs; and yet, by the deposition of three witnesses, it is proved that both were already dead previous to the said year."

Section V.

OTHER AUTHORITATIVE STATEMENTS ON THE SAME ARGUMENT.

ET us conclude this second part by simply remarking:—

1st. That the principal reason for which the Waldenses were punished in Piemont was not precisely their religious belief, but their having been rebellious against the orders of the Sovereign and the laws of the country in which they lived: which is proved, not only by the many facts herein recorded, and sometimes admitted and confessed by the Waldenses themselves, as we have already seen, but also confirmed by the written records of

several public men of the time. We are now going to
quote them. Monsieur Servien, the Ambassador of the
King of France in Turin writes thus to the Governor and
Consul of Fragela: "Turin, April 14, 1655. I write to
you these lines to let you know that his Royal Highness,
being dissatisfied with some inhabitants of the valley of
Lucerne, not only for opposing his orders, but also for
making others directly contrary unto them, by an attempt
full of insolence, hath resolved to have that obedience that
is due unto him." (State Papers of John Thurloe, vol.
III. p. 413. London, 1742.) Let us see also (L. C. p. 578)
what De Lionne, the French Ambassador at Rome, wrote to
Bordeaux, the French Ambassador in England. "Rome,
July 3, 1655: I hope that the pretence which the Protector
(Cromwell) takes to defer the signing of your treaty upon
the business of the valleys of Savoy, will suddenly cease;
since Monsieur Servien, Ambassador for the King at Turin,
hath writ me word, that he hoped to accommodate the same
in a short time, according to the orders which he had received from the Court: although it is not a War for their Religion, but a pure revolt against the Prince." Count Brienne
besides may be heard in his letter written to Bordeaux, the
French Ambassador in England (L. c. p. 817): "Soisson,
July 16, 1655. As for the business of Savoy, . . . you
may assure the Protector that we have done all what he
could desire of us. But we can but entreat and not command the Prince of Savoy. Certain it is that his subjects
had very much forgotten their duty." It is then to over-
throw the historical evidence to say that the Waldenses
were persecuted for their religious opinions.

Second, That, speaking in particular of the famous year
1655, if, on the one hand, we must admit that many Waldenses were killed during the combats at the places which
were attacked or held by the soldiers of the Sovereign; on
the other, it is equally certain, in accordance with the depositions quoted above, that the catalogue of murders, tedious

for their length, and abominable for their indecent and cruel
details, is nothing else than a malicious dream of the excited
imagination of a deceiver. Sir Samuel Morland himself, in
a letter to Thurloe, the Secretary of Cromwell, has the following striking expressions on the subject (State Papers,
vol. III. p. 417); "Geneva, January 15, 1656." As to the
History. . . . I have not neglected to use my utmost dili-
gence, since the verie first time you mentioned the same. . .
The greatest difficulty I meet with is in relation to the
matter of fact in the beginning of these troubles and during
the time of warr. For I find, upon diligent search, that
many papers and bookes which have been put out in print
on this subject, even by some Ministers of the valleys, *are
lame in many particulars and in manie things not conformable
to truth.*" Notable expression not to be forgotten!

Third, That in the said year 1655, the number of the
Waldenses in the valleys of Piemont amounted to about
16,000, as is also admitted by John Leger, and the killed,
both by sword and by fire, and also in their flight, did not
exceed altogether 200 in number, as is stated in the report
published at that time by the Sardinian Government in
Italian, French, and Latin; which was printed also in Morland's History (p. 398). Too many, if the preciousness of
human life is considered; but very few indeed, if compared
with the ordinary history of unsuccessful revolutions, and
with the many thousands of human beings sacrificed on like
occasions, not to speak of other places and times, especially
here in England and Ireland, in the same unhappy seventeenth century.

---

* Here assigned 1656, because the year
1656, printed in the State Papers, &c., is a
mistake. The facts alluded to in this letter
happened not in January, 1656, but in the
following May.

In the same State Papers, &c., it is said
that this Morland's letter was answered by
Lord Ch. Hardwicke, High Chancellor of
Great Britain.

THE RELIGIOUS DOCTRINES OF THE WALDENSES.

SECTION I.

A SKETCH OF THE CHANGES IN THE WALDENSIAN DOCTRINES, FROM THE EARLIEST PERIOD TO THE TIME OF THE NEW REFORMERS.

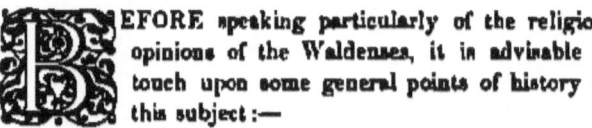

BEFORE speaking particularly of the religious opinions of the Waldenses, it is advisable to touch upon some general points of history on this subject :—

First. That it was a mistake of some writers to accuse the old Waldenses of holding errors which they, as a body, had in abomination. For instance, that they admitted two gods and two principles, the good and the bad, as the Manicheans did ; that they denied Baptism and the other Sacraments ; that they rejected the Apostles' Creed, and permitted promiscuous sexual intercourse, &c. These and many other tenets, sometimes attributed to the old Waldenses, cannot be said with truth to have been their errors, as there is no trace of them in any of the Waldensian manuscripts. I am of opinion that this mistake was caused, either by this, that some of the followers of Peter of Vaudis had belonged at first to other sects of the time, and previously held errors like those, or, that it was the effect of confounding the Waldensian sect with that of the Catharites, or of the Apostolicals, or of the Albigenses. At any rate, we must repeat that the Waldenses, as a particular body of sectarians, were quite free from those abominable and destructive errors.

Second. That they in their outset held nothing at variance with the common doctrines of the Catholic Church, within which they were at first educated, except their preaching and expounding publicly the Holy Scriptures, in spite of the prohibition of the Bishops of the same Church. "The Waldenses" (I quote the words of Neander, in his "History of the Christian Religion and Church," vol. VIII.) "laboured with great zeal, and certainly without any thought at first of separating themselves from the Church; but simply aiming at a spiritual society like many others in the service of the Church." And this is pretty clear to every one who considers the fact that an embassy of their body went to Rome in the year 1179, at the time of the Third Council of Lateran, in order that Pope Alexander the Third would sanction their society, and approve of their book. This point of history is confirmed by the English Franciscan, Walter Mapes, who in that very year was in Rome, and had a conversation with two of the Waldensian embassy, as he relates in his work "De Nugis Curialium," existing among the manuscripts of the Bodleian Library (851) at Oxford. I will quote a few words only of this contemporary : * "We saw Waldensian men in the Roman Council held by Pope Alexander the Third. They were simple and unlearned, and were thus called from the name of their founder, Valdo, who was a citizen of Lyons on the Rhone. They presented to the Pope a book written in the old Provençal language, in which there were texts and comments of the Psalms, and

---

* Vidimus in Concilio Romano sub Alexandro Papa III. calaterato Valdenics homines ydiotas illiteratos, a primate ipsorum Valdo dictus, qui fuerat civis Lugdunensis super Rodanum; qui librum domino Papæ præsentaverunt lingua conscriptum Gallica, in quo textus et glossa Psalterii, plurimorumque Legis Utriusque librorum continebantur. (See note 25).

of many books of the Old and New Testament," &c. It is true that they were sent back without obtaining what they asked, and were forbidden to explain the Scriptures, and to preach publicly in their own way; yet they were not condemned at that time as guilty of any error in doctrine. Besides, when John a Bellismanibus, Archbishop of Lyons, about the year 1182 or 1183, also forbade them both to preach and expound the Scriptures, and finding them disobedient, expelled them from his diocese; no mention was made of their holding any doctrine at variance with the teaching of the Church: they were simply expelled because, being laymen and illiterate, and, of course, frequently using erroneous expressions, presumed, against the prohibition of their superiors, to preach, and exercise an office which was confided to the Apostles and to their successors only. And, in fact, two of the original followers of the Waldensian sect, the one named Durandus of Huesca, who had also been a master of Waldian in a school at Milan; and the other, Bernard Primo, and a great number of their Waldensian companions, having shown their desire to be reunited with the Church, their petition was readily granted by Pope Innocent the Third; and they besides received from him letters and diplomas authorizing them to establish religious orders. The letters to Durandus are of the 18th December, 1208, those to Bernard are dated 14th June, 1210. The two societies, in the year 1256, were united to, and embodied with, the Hermits of St. Augustin (Helyot, " Histoire des Ordres Monastiques." Guingamp, 1839, vol. II. p. 283 et seq.).

Third. Notwithstanding what we have said, it cannot be denied that the Waldenses in after times admitted and professed many articles of doctrine, against the teaching and practices of the Roman Church, as we shall see in separate articles. Yet a very broad distinction is to be drawn between many articles of their religious doctrine in the old time, and those adopted by the new Waldenses after the

appearance of the reformers Luther and Calvin. The latter
are very different from the former in many substantial
points ; so that, if the Waldenses who existed in the
thirteenth and fourteenth century, had risen from their
graves and mingled with those of the seventeenth and
eighteenth, they would have judged the latter very unfaithful to their old religion. Let us read the often quoted
MS. (" Veritable Histoire," p. 2) : " The Waldenses became
Lutheran on the appearance of Luther, and a little afterwards from being Lutheran they became Calvinist. John
Leger, who took upon himself the task of being the historian of the valleys of Piemont, presumed to revive in our
days the name of Waldenses, whose heresy died away about
two centuries ago." (*Idem*, MS. p. 294) : " The first public
Waldensian assembly, called together in the valleys, was
held at Angrogna the 12th September, 1532; at which
there was proposed some kind of religious union between
the Waldenses and the Lutherans. The two *barbas*, George
Morel and Peter Masson, objected strongly to this proposal,
on the ground principally that the Lutheran articles were
more in number than the Waldensian. New letters, however, having been received from Germany, some kind of
union between the two sects was made, in spite of the two
barbas : and this was done at another assembly held in the
valley of San Martin, the 15th August, 1533. Nevertheless, through the cunning of Calvin, who, both personally and
by means of his partizans—principally William Farel—repeatedly addressed the Waldenses, they a few years afterwards gave way, and, in 1536, became Calvinists. Not
totally so, however, at first; because, being obliged by the
Senate of Turin to declare their religious belief, they made
a confession of faith neither in accordance with Luther,
whom they had already abandoned, nor in accordance with
Calvin, whom they did not yet profess to follow entirely.
The profession of their faith presented to the Senate was a
mixture of the two sects. They declared, 1st. That the religion

of their ancestors and their own was that which God has
revealed in the Old and New Testament; 2nd. That it was
summarily contained in the twelve articles of the Creed;
3rd. That they held the Sacraments, not, however, to the
number of seven; 4th. That they received the Four First
General Councils of Nice, Ephesus, Constantinople and
Calcedon, the Athanasian Creed and the Commandments of
Our Lord, as they are written in the books of Exodus and
Deuteronomy; 5th. That they acknowledged the Princes
of the earth; 6th. That after all, they did not consider
themselves under any obligation to obey the Roman Church,
nor of observing her decrees."

M. A. Rorengo ("Esame intorno alla nuova Confessione
di Fede, ecc. Torino, 1658," p. 33) confirms the same Waldensian changes by addressing them thus: "You allow your
confession of faith to run like the fashion of our clothes,
now long, now large, now narrow. Up to the present time
you hold the rule of the First Councils and of the First
Doctors of the Church. Now you cast them aside, and then
place instead the confession of Flanders, Holland, &c. so
that under such rules we are unable to dispute and to dis-
cover what your faith is. Observe (L. c. p. 45) that
St. Augustin acknowledges for a true Church that which
has the succession of Pontiffs and Priests. And you pretend that the new confession lasted from the Apostles, from
St. Peter to *barba* Martini. How can you exhibit successors both in the hierarchical chair, and in the doctrine?"[*]

What has been noted here will show generally that the
Waldenses have undergone some great changes in relation

* *Voi fate correre la vostra confessione di fede con la moda dei vestiti or larghi
or larghi ora stretti. Precedete finora la regola dei primi Concilii e Dottori della
Chiesa. Ora gli levate surrogando la confessione di Fiandra, Olanda ecc.; affinchè
con tali regole non si possan e possa disputare qual sia la vostra fede. Osservate
che Sant' Agostino trova per vera vecra della Chiesa la successione dei Pontefici e
Sacerdoti. E voi volete che la confessione nuova abbia durato dagli Apostoli, da
San Pietro a barba Martini. Come proderete successori nella cattedra e nella
dottrina?.*

to their religious opinions at different epochs, principally after Luther and Calvin. Let us now descend to the particulars.

SECTION II.

THE RELIGIOUS DOCTRINES OF THE OLD WALDENSES WHICH AGREED WITH THOSE OF THE CATHOLIC CHURCH AND DIFFERED FROM THE TENETS OF THE NEW REFORMERS.

JOHN LEGER has printed several confessions of the Waldensian faith, and assigns the first to the year 1120, about sixty or eighty years (he wrongly says) before Valdo of Lyons (1st Part, p. 92 and following). This confession contains fourteen articles. In the third a distinction is made between the Canonical and the Apocryphal books, and the Waldenses are made to say that they read the Apocryphal for the instruction of the people, not, however, for proving by them Ecclesiastical Doctrines; and in the thirteenth article it is stated plainly, that they have not known of any other Sacrament, except Baptism and the Eucharist: "*Nos non aben conegu autre sacrament que lo baptisma e la eucharistia.*"

Not to say anything now about the other four confessions given by this writer, I call the reader's attention to the two recited articles of the first, and remark—First. That no Waldensian confession of faith can be older than the Waldenses themselves. Now there is no doubt that this sect did not arise before the second half of the twelfth century, as has been fully proved in our first part. Second. That, in accordance with Professor James Henthorn Todd (The book of the Vaudois, p. 8 and following), this confession, printed by Leger with the false date of 1120, is in substance and in many parts verbally the same as that which Morel and Masson showed to Oecolampadius and to Bucer in 1530, when the two *barbas* went to consult them on the particulars

of their religion, in order to come to some agreement between themselves. Third. That the division of the books
of the Scriptures into Canonical and Apocryphal, there
stated to have been made by the old Waldenses, and the
admission of two Sacraments only, are points contradicted
by the same old Waldenses in their manuscripts. We have
only to open them and read some passages.

In relation to the different books of the Bible, there is
not to be found in any of the old Waldensian texts either
the word or the signification of the word *Apocryphal.* They
admitted the whole of the Bible as it was admitted by the
Catholics, without excluding from the number of its books
those which by the new reformers are excluded as not
Canonical. In volume C of the Waldensian manuscripts,
in the Cambridge Library, there is a translation of part of
the second of the Maccabees, chapter vii. from the Vulgate,
and a translation of some chapters of Job, and the whole
book of Tobit also from the Vulgate, comprising that
famous passage of the Angel : " Prayer is good with fasting
and alms, more than to lay up treasures of gold ; for alms
delivereth from death, and the same is that which purged
away sins, and maketh to find mercy and life everlasting " [*]
(Tob. chap. xii. 8 and 9). In volume E there are extracts
from Proverbs, Ecclesiastes, and Ecclesiasticus. In volume
F, amongst translations of parts of the New Testament,
there are two chapters of the Book of Wisdom ; and in
volume B there is a treatise on the Commandments.
They are not divided in accordance with the new reformers,
but in accordance with the Catholic Catechism : namely,
the first and second commandment, according to the division
adopted by the reformers, are united and called *the first
commandment,* as the Catholics do. And the commandment
called the tenth by the same reformers, is divided into two,
also in accordance with the division adopted by the Catholic

[*] Bona era lunazion e la briava e lalmoznia majer be a treazaabre rounar far, car lalmoznia triliera be seger car all mortana penga li gura e far a traber luta riveca.

Church. Therefore the Waldenses, in their manuscript, put as the second commandment: Not to take the name of your Lord God in vain—*Le srgont comanbamrnt non prmbrcas lo nome bel la tsegnor Dio rnban;* and put as the ninth, Thou shalt not covet thy neighbour's wife; and as the tenth, Not to covet thy neighbour's goods—*Le noben no cubitace la molher bel tso ppme—Le brcen es no cubitar las cosas bel tos ppme.* What I have stated concerning the Cambridge manuscripts as to the distinction of the Apocryphal books not being found there, but, on the contrary, everything in accordance with the Catholic Bible, is also to be observed of the Waldensian manuscripts in Trinity College, Dublin, of a more recent date; yet previous to the new reformers, in which, according to the positive assertion of Dr. Todd (L. c. p. 4), no distinction is to be found between the Canonical books of the Bible and those called Apocryphal by the reformers: and every Scriptural book or passage is always quoted there in accordance with the Catholic Bible, comprising the controverted passage of St. John (1 Ep. v. 7), which is also written there: "There are three that give testimony in heaven, the Father, the Word, and the Holy Ghost; and these three are One—*Tri son li qual bonan nstimoni al cri lo Paire e la Filh e lo sanct Sprrit, r a quisri tri son un.*" This will be enough to show that the Waldenses, before Luther and Calvin, had their Bible as the Catholics have it now; without excluding the books or the passages excluded by the same Waldenses, after having become Calvinists. It will also demonstrate the falsehood of the date of 1120 given by Leger as that of the first confession of the Waldensian faith.

In relation now to the Sacraments, of which, in that confession of faith attributed by Leger to the beginning of the twelfth century, it is said that the old Waldenses admitted two only, Baptism and the Eucharist; it will be enough to read a few lines of the Cambridge Waldensian MS. In volume D, under the title, "Exposition of Christian Doc-

trine," at chapter ii. there are the following words : "Seven
are the Sacraments of the Holy Church. The first is
Baptism given to us in remission of sins. The second is
Penance. The third is the Communion of the Body and
the Blood of Christ. The fourth is Matrimony ordered by
God. The fifth is Holy Oil (Extreme Unction). The sixth
is the Imposition of Hands (Confirmation). The seventh is
the Ordination of Priests and Deacons." *

In the " Rerum Bohemicarum Antiqui Scriptores ex
Bibliotheca Freheri," &c. (Hanoviæ, 1602), at p. 238, *et seq.*
there is printed that Waldensian Confession of Faith which
was sent to Uladislaus, king of Hungary, in the year 1508.
We find there the following words: " We equally admit
that the Sacraments, which are seven in number, are useful
to the Church of Christ: *Similiter, Sacramenta, Septenario
numero inclusa, Ecclesiæ Christi utilia esse pandimus.*" And
in the next pages, namely, from 241 to 252 (which are evidently cut out in the copy existing in the library of the
British Museum, but are to be seen in the copy of the
Cambridge library), there is an enumeration and explanation of each sacrament. About Baptism, after saying,
that "All grown persons are obliged to be baptized in the
name of the Father, and of the Son, and of the Holy
Ghost," they profess besides, that also infants must be baptized, according to a decree of the Apostles, as Dionysius
writes: *"Professio nostra etiam in pueros extenditur, qui decreto
Apostolorum, ut Dionysius scribit, baptizari debent."* About
the Sacrament of Orders they mention the Major and the
Minor Orders: " *De Sacerdotali Ordine . . . Majores et
Minores Ordines.*" Express mention is made besides of
Extreme Unction of the Sick—" *Unctio Extrema Infor-
morum,*" and of the other Sacraments of " Confirmation, of

* Sept son ti sacramens de la sancta glyeysa. Lo premier es lo batisme, lo
qual es bons a nos en remission de pecca. Lo 2 es la penitencia. Lo 3 es la
comunion del cors e del sang de X.J. Lo 4 es lo matrigoud ordena de Dio. Lo 5
es lo sant ..., Lo 6 es traspausament de las mans. Lo 7 es ordenament de preyres
e de diaques.

Matrimony, of Penance in the Remission of Sins, and of The
Eucharist :—*De Confirmatione, De Matrimonio, De Pœnitentia
lapsorum in Remissionem Peccatorum, De Eucharistia.*" In
explaining the last mentioned Sacrament there are the following striking expressions : " Wheresoever a worthy Priest,
with faithful people, according to his intention and that of
Christ, and according to the ordination of the Church, will
in his prayers testify with such words, namely : ' *This is my
body, This is my blood*,' immediately then the present bread
is the body of Christ, which was offered to death for us ; and
in like manner the present wine is His blood, shed for the
remission of sins. This profession of our faith is founded
on the words of Christ, related by the Evangelists and by
Saint Paul. . . . This body and blood of Christ, under the
species of bread and wine, ought to be received." *

It will not be altogether out of place to note here with
Dr. Todd (L. c. p. 216), that in the Dublin Waldensian
manuscripts there is an instruction to the clergy, headed
thus : "*Sequitur De Imposicione Pœnitentia;*" which imposition of Penance, according to the Catholic doctrine, is an
integral part of the Sacrament of like name; and that some
of the passages published by Perrin, Morland, and Leger
from the Waldensian manuscripts, are not translated faithfully by them. To say nothing about Leger, Perrin, in his
book of the Vaudois, has published the Commandments not
in accordance with the manuscripts from which he states he
copied them; and has divided into two the first, and out of
the two last Commandments has made one. And, as Dr. Todd
says (L. c. p. 116), we are not to consider Perrin's history
of the Vaudois the offspring of a single and solitary *pasteur*

---

* L'bicumque dignus Sacerdos cum fido populo, juxta suam et Christi intentionem
Ecclesiæque ordinationem, orationem forinse, hujusmodi verbis, videlicet : Hoc est
corpus meum, Hic est sanguis meus, testificatus fuerit ; confestim præsens
panis est corpus Christi in mortem pro nobis oblatum ; vinum similiter præsens est
sanguis ejus effusus in peccatorum remissionem. Hæc fidei nostræ professio verbis
Christi firmatur ab Evangelistis et a Sancto Paulo conscriptis. . . . Hoc corpus
Christi et sanguis . . . sub panis vinique speciebus . . . sumi debet.

of Dauphiny, but as the work of the French Protestant Church; and a very curious work too: as it was examined a great many times in many protestant provinces and in Geneve, during the space of more than ten years before it was published in 1619. About Morland we may say that he, besides publishing his history, in accordance with the false views and suggestions of Leger, against his own first conviction (*see* his letter in our Part II. Sect. v.), and besides omitting the publication of passages contained in the manuscripts; which would have been more than sufficient to cast light on the true epoch of the Waldensian sect and doctrines; has taken the liberty of altering a passage, in which the manuscript, commenting upon a text of St. Augustin, says: "Vain fear is it to fear losing the company of father and mother, and not to fear the loss of the company of God and of the Virgin Mary—*La compagnia de Dio e de la Uergena Maria.*" Now Morland (p. 129) translated it thus: "And not to fear losing the blessed presence of God the Father, and of Jesus Christ." (Todd, L. c. p. 99.)

I may be allowed to observe here that the old Waldenses, though they denied the intercession of Saints and of the Virgin Mary (as we shall see afterwards), yet they admitted that honour and praise is due to them. Hear them in the above quoted confession of faith (" Rerum Bohemicar. Freheri," p. 254, 255):* "God is to be praised in his Saints, as David said, 'Praise the Lord in his Saints;' and we are doing so, and praise God in this Virgin, and in the other Saints. Because God in his goodness gave to them like grace and like benefits, and through them to us. And not only we praise God in this Blessed Virgin, but besides we confess her blessed and holy; and we love and imitate her

---

* *In Sanctis Deus laudari debet, sicut dixit David—Laudate Dominum in Sanctis ejus—Et nos hoc agimus quod in hac Virgine et aliis Sanctis Deum laudamus, qui talem gratiam et talia beneficia ex sua bonitate eis dedit et nobis per ipsam. Et nedum in hac beneficia Virgine Deum laudamus, sed et eam confitemur benedictam et benitam, et diligimus et sequimur pro posse nostro ... Nulla ex*

H

as we can. . . . No woman is as holy as this Virgin is.
None indeed is full of grace, except her; none should be
called blessed amongst all generations, except her alone.
Nor is it true that we despise as profane the holy days of the
commemoration of the glorious Virgin Mary; on the contrary we respect them, and sing many canticles concerning
her to the honour of God."

It is therefore beyond doubt that, before the time of
Luther and Calvin, the Waldenses admitted all the books of
the Bible and all the Seven Sacraments as the Catholic
Church did and does now, and that they did not deny the
Real Presence of our Lord after the consecration of the
bread and wine, and paid honour to the Virgin and to the
Saints: and besides (*see* Dr. Todd, L. c. p. 19), from the
doubts proposed in Germany by Morel and Masson, it seems
clear that they approved of Religious Celibacy, Auricular
Confession, Vows of Poverty, &c.

I conclude this article, relating the doctrines of the old
Waldism as distinguished from Calvinism, by quoting three
passages of " La Nobla Leyçon," bearing on the subject.

In the first passage, the Waldensian writer praises the
sincere Confession of sins, and the works of Penance, fasting, alms-giving, fervent praying, as means to obtain salvation:

" To make our Confession sincerely without any defect:
And to do penance during the present life;
To fast, to give alms, and to pray with fervent heart;
Indeed, through these things the soul finds salvation."[?]

In the second, he commends the Evangelical Counsel to

[Foussent se confesent serjn alcun mancament,
E qu' il fasan penitencia en la vita present,
Dejunar, far almoynas et aver lo cor bullent,
Car per aquestas cosas troba l'arma salvament.]

keep Virginity; and Mary and Joseph are quoted as an example of this:

> "The Old Law cursed the womb which remained barren,
> But the New Law commandeth to keep Virginity.
> Our Lady was pure and Joseph also." * [*]

In the third passage is boldly proclaimed that a lawfully contracted marriage is indissoluble under the Gospel.

> "The Old Law gave power to dissolve Marriage,
> And the bill of repudiation was then to be given:
> But the New Law says: Do not marry one that is put away;
> And what God hath joined together, let no man put asunder." [†]

---

* La ley vuilla maudi lo ventre que fova aon a porta,
Ma la noberlla caurtilla garbar vergenena.
Nora fra nostra tona e Joseph aucaí.

† La ley aneona al partio lo matrimoni :
E cant lo rubo se lengarava benni :
Ma la noberlla ta non pren la leya :
E neugora non torporta so que Dio ha cioun.

---

* The Waldenses hold also here the old Catholic doctrine, not only about the virginity of Mary, but also about the chastity of St. Joseph. The opinion of the Helvidians, who professed that Mary, after Jesus Christ, had other sons by St. Joseph, was condemned amongst other old heretics. (See St. Aug. de Hæresib. cap. 84; see also Jerome contra Helvidium.) But, as in the Gospels are mentioned the brothers of Jesus Christ called sons of Mary; many old writers were misled into erroneously asserting that the so-called brothers of our Lord, if not children of the Virgin Mary, at least were children of Joseph, born to him previously by another wife. I have said erroneously, because, besides the known custom of the Jews, often mentioned in the Bible, to call their cousins or other near relations by the name of brethren; that assertion is evidently shown to be false by reading the different Evangelists. Read. first St. Matthew (c. xiv. v. 55): "Is not this the carpenter's son? Is not his mother called Mary, and his brethren James and Joseph, and Simon and Jude?" Read now Matthew (c. xxvii. v. 55): "Was Mary Magdalene and Mary the mother of James and Joseph." And see Mark (c. xv. v. 40): "Among whom was Mary Magda-

lene and Mary the mother of James the less and of Joseph." Let us turn now to St. John (c. xix. v. 25): "Now there stood by the cross of Jesus his mother, and his mother's sister Mary the wife of Cleophas, and Mary Magdalene." Now, if the different passages are considered together, it will appear by the best evidence that Mary, sister of the Mother of Jesus, wife of Cleophas, is the mother of James (the less) and of Joseph, who, with Simon and Jude, are called brethren of our Lord: but, being the sons of the sisters of his mother and of Cleophas (not of St. Joseph), they were not his brethren in fact; they were his cousins only. In support of the present point I will add the authority of St. Jerome (Comm. in c. xii. St. Matthew): "As is contained" (he says) "in the book which we have written against Helvidius, we understand that the expression, brethren of our Lord, means not the sons of Joseph, but the cousins of our Saviour, sons of Mary, aunt of our Lord, who is styled the mother of James and Joseph and Jude." Now, sicut in libro, quem contra Helvidium scripsimus, continetur, fratres Domini, non filios Joseph sed consobrinos Salvatoris, Mariæ liberæ intelligimus materteræ Domini; quæ esse dicitur mater Jacobi et Joseph et Judæ.

Section III.

THE RELIGIOUS TENETS OF THE OLD WALDENSES AGREEING WITH THOSE OF THE NEW REFORMERS, AND AT VARIANCE WITH THE CATHOLIC DOCTRINES.

NO one will, I think, expect that I should treat here of those religious opinions of the Waldenses which they adopted after they became Calvinists. It would take me out of my subject, and oblige me to enter into too wide a field. Nevertheless, in fulfilment of the task I have undertaken, it is requisite that I should speak here of those tenets which the Waldenses held as a particular body of sectarians, before they united and made a common profession with the new reformers. It will appear from the following particulars, that the new reformers had a good reason to regard the old Waldenses as their ancestors, because nearly all the points, in which the Waldenses during three centuries disagreed from the Roman Church, were likewise assumed and kept by the new reformers, although with a good many additions of their own.

To proceed on safe ground in this rather perplexing investigation, I will take for my guide the Waldensian manuscripts, and those old authors who wrote on this subject, from the end of the twelfth to the beginning of the sixteenth century, that is to say, from the first spreading of the Waldensian sect to nearly the time in which they united with Calvin. These authors, in order of time, are Bernard, Abbot of Chaude Fontaine, the Venerable F. Moneta, Reinerius Sacco, Peter Pilichdorff, Eneas Sylvius, afterwards Pius II., Seyssell, Archbishop of Turin, and Rerum Bohemicarum Scriptores. In the first part of this book they have been quoted, with the dates and places in which they were published, or where those in MS. are preserved. Thus, without any interruption, I shall be able

to recapitulate here the principal Waldensian tenets as they
are expressed by the Waldenses themselves, or by the above-
named authors; and I will subjoin immediately in a few
words, the Catholic doctrine on the same point, in order to
show that the Waldensian tenets are contrary to the Catholic
doctrine, as well as consonant to that of the new reformers.

§ 1.

WALDENSIAN TENET.

The Church of God has failed.

" The Waldenses say that the Church of God failed at the
time of Pope Silvester, and that it was restored in their
time, and that the first restorer was Waldenius." (Moneta,
lib. v. ch. iii.)*

" You quote the words of our Lord (Matth. xx. 16),
'Many are called but few are chosen,' where you say that
the many called express the Catholics, and the few chosen
express your associates." (Pilichdorff, chap. xiv.)†

‡ " That part of the Church, which remained faithful " (at
the time of Constantine), "persevered for a long time in the
received truth. Thus little by little, the holiness of the
Church failed . . . . And thus we believe, that from the time
at which the Church was founded, to the end of the world,

---

* Isti hæretici dicunt Ecclesiam Dei tempore Beati Silvestri defecisse: in temporibus autem istis restitutam esse asserunt per ipsos, quorum primus fuit Val-
denius. (Moneta.)

† Sed objicis verbum Domini (Matth. xx. 16): Multi sunt vocati, pauci
vero electi; ubi per vocatos et multos intelligis Catholicos, et per paucos electos intelligis complices tuos. (Pilichdorff.)

‡ Æt la part permanens permana pri mod crey en sequela verим la cal ilp ma
mcrupu. Guayd la sanctitu de la gleysa manque per a par. . . . C caypd coven
que tei crom ai cai la gleyas fo fama fatte a la fin del argir, la gleysa de Deu nen

she shall not so fail that some holy man be not left on earth, or in some country of the earth. . . . O beloved, consider that the Moon, though nearly losing her fulness, yet she always is substantially the same Moon. And if she is obscured through some darkness, and does not appear to the eyes of men, yet she continues to be the Moon in her substance, as we believe; otherwise God every month should create a Moon. And the Moon often is a figure of the Church." (The Waldensian MSS. of Cambridge, vol. A, fol. 237, 239, 240.)

CATHOLIC DOCTRINE ON THIS POINT.

The Church of the New Testament cannot fail, either by disappearing, or by remaining concealed with a few followers, or by teaching errors against the revealed doctrine in relation to faith and morals.[*]

[Latin footnote text, largely illegible] . . . O Waldensian, . . . (Waldensian MSS.)

---

[*] The Catholics support this doctrine by that saying in Luke (ch. I, v. 32, 33): "The Lord God shall give to him (to our Redeemer) the throne of David his father, and he shall reign in the house of Jacob for ever; and of his kingdom there shall be no end." And by that revelation made to Daniel (ch. ii, v. 44): "The God of heaven shall set up a kingdom that shall never be destroyed . . . , and itself shall stand for ever." Besides, by quoting the words of our Saviour to Peter (Matth. xvi. 18): "Upon this rock I will build my Church, and the gates of hell shall not prevail against it;" and His saying to the Apostles (ch. xxviii. 20): "I am with you always, even to the end of the world;" and the authority of St. Paul (1 Timothy iii. 15): "The House of God, the pillar and ground of truth;" the Catholics, on the strength of these and other authorities, conclude that the Church of God on earth cannot fail either by disappearing and remaining concealed with a few followers, or by teaching errors against faith or morals.

§ 2.

WALDENSIAN TENET.

No other prayer is to be said except the Lord's Prayer, &c.

" The Waldenses say, that no other prayer is to be said except the ' Our Father,' and that all other prayers, which are said or read in the Mass, are not of Divine institution, but of men, the words of Consecration and the ' Our Father ' alone excepted." (Pilichdorff, ch. xxix.)*

CATHOLIC DOCTRINE.

If the Waldenses mean to say that we are not allowed to utter any other prayer in supplicating God, except the identical prayer of the " Our Father " and the words of the Consecration at the Mass, they are mistaken."

---

* *Dicunt Valdenses nihil aliud orandum esse quam Pater Noster ; et quod omnia alia quæ dicuntur et leguntur in Missa non sint Institutionis Divinæ sed humanæ, solis verbis Consecrationis et Pater Noster exceptis.* (Pilichdorff).

" The Catholics admit that the words of Consecration and the Lord's Prayer are undoubtedly of Divine institution, yet they maintain that Christ is done and follow that all other prayers are of no use; and say that there are many other prayers besides to be very much respected and used, principally those contained in the Liturgies and Rituals of the Church, part of which are transmitted to us from the very time of the Apostles, or their first Disciples ; as is the case with the three famous Liturgies called of St. Peter or Missa Romana, of St. Mark or Alexandrina, and of St. James the cousin of our Lord, called of Jerusalem : which last Liturgy is quoted (Catech. & Mystagogy) by St. Cyril of Jerusalem, who flourished the year 350.

§ 3.

WALDENSIAN TENET.

The Holy Scriptures alone are sufficient to guide men to Salvation.

" We shall first briefly say that the Law of the true God is by itself sufficient for the salvation of all the human generation, and it is a Law of perfect liberty, which it is not right to add any thing to, or to take away any thing from, and that there is not any kind of good which is not sufficiently comprised in the same His Law." (Waldensian MSS. Cambridge, vol. D. Prol. of Chr. Doctr.)*

The Waldenses despise all those approved practices of the Church, which they do not see written in the Gospel. *Omnes consuetudines Ecclesiæ approbatas, quas in Evangelio non legunt, contemnunt.* (Reinerius Sacco).*

---

* Deum proprierement une lextra byraerent teaux la top tri teraç Dia e tereç team 3 b Et prr et outa et autriet a le mis de toca la gruturigen puremen, e ee plus bree e plus comuna e plus legicra e complts, e ee try de perirtis tibran, e la qual pen brengen sleguets ai terraer sirpula caan, e nan ee alrana cana de teru la qual tun sia eutairaturre curtum ru aturtis teteyun sun try. (*Waldenrian MSS.*)

---

* The Waldenses, as well as the old Marionais and the Pelagians, grounded this tenet on the following passages (Deut. iv. 3): " You shall not add to the word that I speak to you, neither shall you take away from it." (Matth. xv. 6): " And you have made void the commandment of God for the sake of your traditions;" and (Colos. ii. 8): " Beware, lest any man cheat you by philosophy and vain deceit, according to the tradition of men."

CATHOLIC DOCTRINE ON THIS SUBJECT.

Besides the Holy Scriptures, the Traditions of the Church are to be admitted, without which both the existence and the meaning of the Holy Scriptures would be uncertain, and many things necessary to salvation would be defective."

" The Catholics quote the authority of St. Paul, commanding (2 Thess. ii. 14) to keep the Traditions received either by word or by writing : " Brethren, stand fast and hold the Traditions which you have learned, whether by word or by our Epistle." And with St. Basil (who flourished the year 350), they are persuaded that, " The dogmas which are held and preached in the Church are derived partly from the written Doctrine, and partly from the Apostolical Tradition mysteriously brought to us, and that both have the same claim on our pious respect." *Quod utroque eundem ac pietatem vim habent.* And conclude by saying that, without admitting the Tradition of the Church, we could not be certain that the Holy Scriptures contain the unadulterated Word of God, nor of their real meaning, neither of the articles of the Creed, and of many dogmas and practices of our Christian belief, which are either explained or defined simply through Tradition.

In relation to the passages quoted above (note 44) the Catholics observe that the first passage has relation simply to the legal and ceremonial observances of the Jews ; that the second tells against the deceitful traditions of the elders opposed to the law of God ; and that the third condemns the accretions of the Gentiles in opposition to the Christian religion.

§ 4.

WALDENSIAN TENET.

**The Blessings and Consecrations practised in the
Church do not confer any particular sanctity
upon the things or persons blessed or consecrated.**

" The Waldenses equally condemn the consecration of the
vestments of the Priests, of water, salt, ashes, candles, palms,
food ; and also the consecration of Bishops, Priests, churches,
altars, cemeteries, baptismal water, unctions with chrism
and oil, &c.; saying that the objects thus consecrated do not
receive any particular sanctity from those words, though
the words by themselves are holy and good." (Pilichdorff,
ch. XXII.)*

---

* *Reprobant Valdenses heretici consecrationes vestium Sacerdotalium, aquæ,
salis, cinerum, candelarum, palmarum, ciborum et etiam consecrationes Episcoporum, Sacerdotum, Ecclesiarum, Altarium, Cæmeteriorum, aquæ Baptismalis, Chris-
matis et Olii Unctionum etc.; dicentes, res illas taliter consecratas nihil omnino
singularis sanctitatis ex illis verbis percipere, licet verba in se sancta sint et bona.*
(Pilichdorff.)

CATHOLIC DOCTRINE.

To say that the blessings and consecrations used in the Church do not confer any particular sanctity, is to deny the most clear authority both of Scripture and of Tradition.[*]

---

[*] The Catholics confirm their doctrine with the authority, 1st, of Exodus (ch. xxix. 21): "And when thou (Moses) hast taken of the blood that is upon the altar, and of the oil of unction, thou shalt sprinkle Aaron and his vesture, his sons and their vestments; and after they and their vestments are consecrated." And (chap. xl. v. 9, et seqq.): "Thou shalt take the oil of unction and anoint the tabernacle with its vessels, that they may be sanctified .... Thou shalt consecrate all with the oil of unction, that they may be most holy." 2ndly, Further, with the fact related in the Acts of the Apostles (viii. 17): "Then they (Peter and John) laid their hands upon them, and they (thus newly baptised) received the Holy Ghost." And again (xi. xii. 6): "And when Paul imposed his hands upon them, the Holy Ghost came upon them." And with the expression of St. Paul (2 Timothy i. 6): "I admonish thee that thou stir up the grace of God which is in thee by the imposition of my hands." Equally with the same, St. Paul (1 Timothy iv. 4, 5): "Every creature of God is good, and nothing is to be rejected that is received with thanksgiving; for it is sanctified by the words of God and prayers." And with St. James (v. 14, 15): "Is any one sick among you? Let him bring in the Priests of the Church, and let them pray over him, anointing him with oil in the name of the Lord, and the prayer of faith shall save the sick man." 3rdly, With the Liturgy of the Church, and the sayings of the Fathers of the first centuries of Christianity. St. Cyrillus, Catech. iii; St. Cyprian, Ep. xii. bk. i.; St Augustin in Julian, bk. vi. cap. viii.; St. Basil de Sp. S. cap. xxvii., &c.

§ 5.

WALDENSIAN TENET.

The Catholic Priests, being all bad, have no authority; and the Pope of Rome is the chief of all heresiarchs.

" The Waldenses are against the Church of Rome and the Sovereign Pontiff, and against all Prelates. (Reinerius Sacco).*

" They say that the Pope is the chief of the heresiarchs." (Pilichdorff, ch. xvi).†

" They state openly that no subjection is due to Priests, nor to the same Sovereign Pontiff, because, being wicked and not imitating the life of the Apostles, they do not possess any Divine authority, and that in consequence they have no power to absolve from sins." (Arch. Seymsell, sheet vii.)‡

---

* *Valdenses sunt contra Ecclesiam Romanam et Summum Pontificem et omnes Prælates.* (Sacco.)

† *Dicunt Papam esse caput heresiarcharum.* (Pilich.)

‡ *Sacerdotibus minime parendum esse prædicant, ne Summo Pontifici quidem; quippe qui, eo quod mali sunt nec Apostolorum ritum imitantur, nullam habent a Deo auctoritatem. Dimittendorum peccatorum nullam Sacerdotes nostros potestatem habere.* (Seymell.)

CATHOLIC DOCTRINE.

The authority of the consecrated Ministers of religion depends upon their ordination and the institution of our Lord, and not upon their behaviour as men: and the Pope of Rome is the successor of St. Peter, and the visible chief and ruler of the Universal Church. [a]

---

[a] The Catholic argue that, as the personal goodness of a layman does not confer on him the character of the Priesthood, so the personal wickedness of a particular Priest, though bringing condemnation to himself, yet does not take away from him the authority of his office: that, if the Waldensian opinion were admitted, no one could be certain even to have been regenerated through Baptism. About the name of Hierarch given to the Roman Pontiff, also in the Waldensian MSS.; on the ground of the Tradition of the Church, reported by Tertullian ("De Præscript."), Origen (apud "Euseb. Histor." lib. iii. cap. 3), Saint Athanasius ("Ux fuga eru," and in "Ep. ad Felicem Papam"), Cyprian ("De Unit. Eccl." and lib. i. Ep. viii. ad Pleben), Jerome ("Ep. E. ad Damasum"), Ambrose (in cap. iii. ad Tim.), Chrysostom ("Ep. ad Innocent. Papam"), Augustin ("Ep. contra Manich. cap. xiv," and "Ep. clii. ad Donat."); and principally by Irenæus (Adversus hæreses, lib. iii. cap. 1 et 3); the Catholics profess the contrary: and in accordance with the General Council of Florence, held with the concurrence of the Eastern Church, the year 1439, under Eugenius IV. they maintain that the Pope of Rome is the Chief and Primate of the Church all through the world; that he is the successor of Peter and the Vicar of Christ, with all power of feeding, ruling, and governing the Universal Church, &c. ("Concil." tom. xxxii., Parisiis, 1644). Diffinimus sanctam Apostolicam Sedem et Romanum Pontificem, in universum orbem terræ primatum, et ipsum Pontificem Romanum successorem esse beati Petri principis Apostolorum, et verum Christi Vicarium, totiusque Ecclesiæ caput, et omnium Christianorum patrem et doctorem existere: et ipsi in beato Petro pascendi, regendi et gubernandi universalem Ecclesiam a Domino nostro Jesu Christo plenam potestatem traditam esse: quemadmodum etiam in gestis Œcumenicorum Conciliorum, et sacris canonibus continetur.

§ 6.

WALDENSIAN TENET.

Everybody has the right to preach publicly the word of God.

" The Waldenses say that the preaching of the Word of God is freely allowed to everybody." (Æneas Sylvius.)[*]

" They all preach indiscriminately, and without any distinction of condition, age or sex." (Bernard Abbot Fontis Calidi.)[†]

CATHOLIC DOCTRINE.

The public preaching of the Word of God is not allowed to persons not duly authorized by the Church; and it is forbidden to women by St. Paul.[a]

---

[*] *Dixul Valdenses liberam cuique praedicationem verbi Dei potere.* (Æneas Sylvius.)

[†] *Praedicant omnes passim, et sine delecto conditionis, aetatis et sexus.* (Abbas Fontis Calidi.)

---

[a] The Catholics, with Bernard, Abbot of Church Fountain, a contemporary of Peter Waldensis, observe, that the Apostles did not preach of their own authority, but they were sent by our Lord; and that St. Paul (Rom. x.) clearly said, that no body is allowed to preach unless he be sent by the legitimate Prelates of the Church; respecting whom he says (ad Hebr. xiii.), " Obey your Prelates and be subject to them." And the same Apostle speaks of the women thus (1 Cor. xiv.): " Let women keep silence in the Churches . . . . for it is a shame for a woman to speak in the Church." They observe besides with St. Peter (Eph. ch. 1.), that " No prophecy of Scripture is made by private interpretation, for the holy men of God spake inspired by the Holy Ghost."

§ 7.

WALDENSIAN TENET.

Every person living, according to the precepts of the Apostles, has authority to hear Confessions.

" The Waldenses say that all Christians, without any distinction, have authority to hear Confessions, provided that they live in accordance with the precepts of the Apostles." (Arch. Seyssell.)*[1]

CATHOLIC DOCTRINE.

Nobody has authority to hear Sacramental Confessions or give Absolution of Sins, except Priests who possess lawful jurisdiction.[2]

---

* *Dicunt Valdenses, Confessionem audiendarum auctoritatem Christianis quavis omnibus, qui secundum Apostolorum præcepta ambulant, esse communem.* (Seyssell.)

---

[1] This Waldensian tenet was probably founded on that passage of St. James (v. 14, 16): "Confess therefore your sins one to another, and pray for one another."

[2] The Catholics say, that if the abovementioned passage of St. James applies to the Sacramental Confession, it is to be understood as relating only to the Priests of the Church mentioned a little before by the same Apostle; and they said, that the power of forgiving sins was given by our Lord, not to all his disciples, but to the Apostles, and to their persons to their legitimate successors only.

§ 8.

WALDENSIAN TENET.

Every Oath is a mortal sin.

" The Waldenses also say that every oath, although taken in a court of justice and with truth, is a sin, and to be condemned." (Pilichdorff.)[*]

" It is another error that they say that every oath is a mortal sin." (Seyssell.)[†]

CATHOLIC DOCTRINE.

Oaths taken with due deliberation and in the interest of truth and justice, are praiseworthy, in accordance with Jeremiah (ch. iv.): "Thou shalt swear, as the Lord liveth, in truth and in judgment and in justice."[*]

---

[*] *Item dicunt Valdenses quod omne juramentum, quantumcumque judicialiter et veridice factum, sit peccatum et reprobatum.* (Pilichdorff.)

[†] *Alius error quo dicunt omne juramentum esse peccatum mortale.* (Arch. Seyssell.)

[†] This opinion of the Waldenses is founded on that saying of our Lord (Matth. v.): "But I say to you, Swear not at all . . . let your speech be yea, yea, nay, nay, and whatsoever is more than this, cometh of evil."

[*] The Catholics understand this expression of our Lord in this sense only, that we are not allowed to swear rashly and imprudently; and that our taking oaths by the name of God is also blameable, when it is to a falsehood, or without due consideration, or for an unjust cause. But at the same time, the Catholics maintain that it is a mistake to say that every oath is absolutely and unconditionally forbidden. Because St. Paul says (Heb. vi.), that " An oath for confirmation is the end of all . . . controversy." And the same Apostle swore saying (ad Rom. i.), "God is my witness, whom I serve." And not only the angel in the Apocalypse (ch. x. 6), "Swore by Him that liveth for ever and ever;" but also our Lord often swore in the Gospels. And in Deuteronomy (ch. vi.) is thus prescribed: " Thou shalt fear the Lord thy God . . . and thou shalt swear by his name."

§ 9.

WALDENSIAN TENET.

Every lie is a mortal sin.

" Another error of the Waldenses is their saying that every lie is a mortal sin." (Arch. Seymell).*

CATHOLIC DOCTRINE.

Though every lie is a fault, yet there are lies which do not make men guilty of a mortal sin.

---

* *Alius error quo Valdenses asserunt, omne mendacium esse peccatum mortale.* (Arch. Seymell.)

---

§ 10.

WALDENSIAN TENET.

Purgatory is a dream, an invention of the sixth century.

"Therefore the Scripture says, and we must believe it,
  That all the men of the world will go through two roads:
  The good will go into glory, the wicked to torments."
                                          (*La Nobla Leyçon.*)*

"As there is not any express mention of such place as Purgatory in any passage of the Law, nor have the Apostles left to us any express instruction about it, nor has the primitive Church, acting in accordance with the Gospel, left to us any order or command about the same; and only after the year of our Lord five hundred and fifty-eight Pope Pelagius gave an order that a commemoration for the dead should be made in the Mass; it remains that there is not any obligation to believe as an article of faith that after this life there is such a place as Purgatory." (**Lo Purgatori soima.** The dream of the Purgatory. Waldensian Treatise).†

"In this article of Purgatory the Barbas of the Waldenses go astray very much, because they say that the departed souls are immediately either brought to eternal joy or

---

* [illegible text]
  [illegible text]
  [illegible text]
                                          (*La Nobla Leyçon.*)

† [illegible text in degraded print]
  [illegible text]
  [illegible text]
  [illegible text]
  [illegible text]
  [illegible text] (*Lo Purgatori soima.
  Waldensian Treatise.*)

plunged into everlasting torments; and [*] that Purgatory is a fiction invented by the avarice of the Clergy." (Arch. Seywell).*

CATHOLIC DOCTRINE.

The existence of Purgatory has been always believed in the Church of God, and it is an article of Christian faith.[*]

* *In suo articulo (de Purgatorio) Valdensium Barba asserunt asserunt . . . . nisul enim defunctorum animas ad cœlum vel gaudia vel supplicia . . . confestim verisâ, exclamationesque eius cupiditate excessive Purgatorium conspicue. (Arch. Seywell.)*

[Footnote left column:]
[*] While believing with the Church that there are only two eternal places, the one prepared for the friends, the other for the enemies of God, heaven and hell; the Catholics hold with the same Church that there is a third place in the next world, called Purgatory, where all persons, who die in the grace of God, but not having yet made sufficient penance for their sins already pardoned in relation to their guilt, are sent to be punished, till they, having perfectly satisfied the justice of God, are admitted to heaven.

[*] As to the assertion, that "No such place as Purgatory has been known in the primitive Church," the Catholics, besides mentioning some passages of St. Matth. (chap. xii.), and of St. Paul (1 Cor. chap. iii. &c.), quote the twelfth chapter of the second book of the Maccabees. The first and the second book of this name are acknowledged as Canonical by the Catholic Church, though they are not in the Canon of the Jews, as it was written under Esdras, namely, long before the existence of the Maccabees. Now we read therein that "Judas making a gathering, sent twelve thousand drachms of silver to Jerusalem for sacrifices to be offered for the sins of the dead." And that, "It is therefore a holy and wholesome thought to pray for the dead, that they may be loosed from sins." Upon which passage St. Augustin thus remarks ("De cura pro Mortuis," cap. L): "We read in the books of the Maccabees, that a sacrifice was offered for the dead. Yet though nothing of this kind could be read in the old Scriptures, not light is the authority of the Universal Church, which is openly famous for this practice; where the commemoration for the dead has its place amongst the prayers

[Footnote right column:]
of the Priests, which are offered to our Lord at his altar." *In Maccabæorum libris legimus oblatum pro mortuis sacrificium. Sed, etsi nusquam in Scripturis veteribus omnino legeretur, non parvæ est Universæ Ecclesiæ, quæ in hac consuetudine claret auctoritas; ubi in precibus Sacerdotis, quæ Domino Deo ad ejus altare funduntur, locum habet etiam commendatio mortuorum.* The Catholics quote besides the old Liturgies and a great number of Fathers of the Church, some of whom flourished in the very first centuries of Christianity, and all previous to the time of the Popes Pelagius and Gregory the Great. They are all speaking of the sufferings for the souls of the dead, they mention the purging fire, and some of them expressly say, that this belief has been taught by the Apostles (see Tertull. "De corona Militis," cap. iii.; Origen, "Hom. 12 in Hierem;" St. Cyrill of Jerusm. "Catech. 5 Mystag. acie medicum;" St. Cyprian, Ep. lxvi., and very often St. Augustin. I will only quote St. Chrysostom (Hom. ii. in Epst. ad Philip.). "It is and without reason, that by the Apostles it has been prescribed that, during the celebration of the venerable mysteries, a commemoration be made of those who departed from us. The Apostles knew that thence they should obtain a great enablement, a great advantage . . . How should we not appease God by praying for them." *Non frustra ab Apostolis sancitum, ut in celebratione reverendorum Mysteriorum memoria fiat eorum qui hinc discesserunt. Noverunt, illis salutem hinc conducturam fieri, multam utilitatis . . . . Quomodo Deum non placaremus pro istis orantes?*

§ 11.

WALDENSIAN TENET.

The Indulgences of the Church are an invention of covetous Priests.

"The Waldenses equally condemn the Indulgences of the Prelates of the Church." (Pilichdorff).[*]

"They affirm that Indulgences are an invention of bad Priests, in order to extort money from the ignorant." (Arch. Seyssell).[†]

CATHOLIC DOCTRINE.

The power of granting Indulgences is not derived from any invention of man, but from the authority given by our Lord to the Church.[*]

---

[*] *Item reprobant Valdenses Indulgentias Prelatorum Ecclesie.* (Pilichdorff.)

[†] *Ipsi affirmant . . . Indulgentias esse inventas a paralentrreddatibus ad extorquendas ab imperitis pecunias.* (Arch. Seyssell.)

[*] The Waldenses enjoy the reputation of having made the first attack upon Indulgences. Wickliff, Huss, Luther, Melancthon, and principally Calvin, distinguished themselves by dwelling on the same doctrine; but we do not know of any body of reformers who had taken their stand against Indulgences before the Waldenses. Pilichdorff (cb. xxx.) admits that the Waldenses and many Catholics of his time doubted about the value of Indulgences by reason of the indiscreet premises of the collectors of alms: *Hæc facit indiscreta pronunciatio questorum seu Nervolorum, qui indifferenter omnibus homicidias hæc et illud facientibus Indulgentias promittunt.* However, the same author adds that these assertions and promises were made against the intention of the Pope and of the Prelates of the Church, who do not grant Indulgences to everybody, but only to those who are truly penitent, who confess and are contrite: *Sit hoc non est nostre Ecclesie Pape et aliorum Prelatorum, qui non dant nisi vere penitentibus et confessis et contritis.*

[*] The Catholic doctrine about Indulgences is this, that when our Lord said to His Apostles (Matth. xviii.): " Whatsoever you shall . . . loose upon earth shall be loosed also in heaven;" He gave to the first Prelates of the Church the power of remitting to the penitent man, under some conditions, the temporal penalties due for the sins already pardoned in relation to their guilt, but not yet atoned by the necessary satisfaction to the justice of God. And beginning with the pardon given by St. Paul to the penitent man of Corinth (2 Cor. ii.), and continuing with the pardon granted by the Church to repentant sinners, at the request and through the intervention of those who had suffered or were suffering for their faith; the Catholics conclude by saying Indulgences granted from ancient times to those who visited on some stated days, particular Churches or holy places, or performed some prescribed pious works, centuries and centuries before the Waldenses rose against them.

§ 12.

WALDENSIAN TENET.

There is no obligation to fast, nor to keep holy
any day, Sunday excepted.

" Another error of the Waldenses is to reprove religious
abstinence." (Arch. Seyssell, sheet LXXIII.).*

" No day is to be kept holy, except Sunday." (Eneas
Sylvius, " Hist. Bohem.") †

Remarks : To fast and to keep holy some particular days
in the week are laws of the Church. Therefore the united
assertions of the Waldenses may be considered as corollaries
to that tenet, in which they maintained that the Prelates of
the Church, being all wicked, have no authority, and that in
consequence their precepts are not binding. Yet the Waldenses did not condemn voluntary mortifications, &c. as we
have seen before.

CATHOLIC DOCTRINE.

All Christians are obliged to keep holy, not only
the Sundays, but also all other particular days
appointed by the authority of the Church; and to
fast and abstain on some other days, according to
the ordinances of the same Church, if there is no
good reason to be exempted. There may be quoted
here St. Augustin, ("Ad Januarium," Epis. 118. 2),
saying, that St. Ambrose told him thus: "When I
go to Rome I fast on the Sabbath day, when I am
here (in Milan) I do not fast. You do the same.
Keep the custom of the Church of that place in
which you are." *Cum Romam venio jejuno Sabbato, quum
hic sum non jejuno. Sic etiam tu, ad quam forte Ecclesiam
veneris, ejus morem serva.*

---

* Alius error Valdensium quo improbant jejunia. (Arch. Seyssell.)
† Nulla dies ab opere cessandum, nisi Dominica, (Eneas Sylvius).

§ 13.

WALDENSIAN TENET.

The Invocation of Saints cannot be admitted.

" Now, it is to be said of the Invocation of Saints, which (the Catholics) publish as it were an article of faith, saying that the Saints existing in heaven are to be prayed to by us who live. . . . And this does not appear worthy of belief." (Waldensian Treatise).*

" They hold that the blessed Virgin Mary and the Saints of heaven are not to be invoked by us, because they cannot pray for us. . . . They do not say the 'Hail Mary.' " (Pilichdorff).†

" They say that mortals are not in need of their intercession, Christ alone being more than sufficient to do everything for us all ; and the Saints absorbed in the delights of their felicity do not know what is passing here below " (Arch. Seyssell).‡

---

* Sen to a ticu ta l'invocation de li sanct, la qual publican como per article de fe, disenti que li sanct existant en la mayria celestial son d'rears prega la nos vivent. . . . Et aizo non es bint razon de creyre. (Waldensian Treatise.)

† Tenent Beatam Virginem et Sanctos in patriâ non esse invocandos a nobis, quia non possunt orare pro nobis . . . Non dicunt 'Ave Maria.' (Pilichdorff.)

‡ Dicunt Sanctorum . . . suffragiâ mortales non indigere, Christo omnibus ad omnia abunde sufficiente. . . . Et Sanctos eos quia in sæculo sunt ignorare, tanta felicitatis illius amænitate capti. (Arch. Seyssell.)

CATHOLIC DOCTRINE.

It is good and useful to have recourse to the intercession of Saints, and all persons who condemn this practice are out of the pale of the Church.[a]

" The Catholic teaching on the invocation of Saints is not precisely that expressed by the quoted Waldensian tenet. The definition of the Church does not say that the Saints of heaven are to be prayed to by us; as though any Christian, who dare not pray through the Saints, were a transgressor against the prescription of the Church. She only says that the invocation of Saints is good and useful in accordance with the Tradition and the written doctrine of the Old and New Testament. The condemnation, therefore, of the Catholic Church is only against those who say that the Saints are not to be invoked; that they do not pray for us; that their invocation is an idolatry against the Word of God, and against our only Mediator Jesus Christ, &c. (see Council of Trent, sess. 25, *Decr. de invocatione, veneratione, &c. Sanctor.*) The Catholics, while invoking the Angels and Saints, and Mary the mother of Christ, do not mean any thing else than to have them as intercessors with our Lord, from whom alone every good gift and grace comes upon men.

§ 14.

Every honour given in the Church to the holy
Images or paintings, and to the relics of Saints
is to be abolished.

"The Antichrist makes the people idolaters: he deceit-
fully causes them to serve the idols of all the world under
the name of Saints and of relics. . . . He causes the worship of Latria, due only to God, to be given to men, male
and female Saints parted from this world, and to their images,
noisome corpses, relics." (Waldensian Treatise on the Antichrist.)[*] [**]

"The Waldenses say that the Images and Pictures are to
be abolished." (Reinerius Sacco.)[†]

"They say that Christians are idolaters by reason of
Images and the Cross." (Pilichdorff.)[‡]

---

[*] Le antichrist te rendent le peuple, servir frauduleusement a les idoles de
cet le monde sur li ment et a las reliquias. . . . De latria a li donne servir a seculars
creatures d'aquest mond, et a las imagenas de lor, sulas, reliquias. (Waldensian
Treatise "de Antichrist.")

[†] Imagines et Picturae dicunt esse abolendas. (Reinerius Sacco.)

[‡] Dicunt Christianos esse idololatras propter Imagines et Signum Crucifixi.
(Pilichdorff.)

[**] Some ground for this Waldensian tenet
is to be found in Deuteronomy (ch. v.), and
in Exodus (ch. xx.), where it is said: "Thou
shalt not make to thyself a graven thing, nor
the likeness of any things that are in heaven
above, or that are in the earth beneath, or
that abide in the water under the earth.
These shalt not adore them, and thou shalt
not serve them. For I am the Lord thy
God, a jealous God."

CATHOLIC DOCTRINE.

The religious honour given in the Church to holy images and paintings, and to the relics of Saints, is in accordance with the revelation of the Bible and ancient Tradition, and has nothing to do with idolatry."

" The Catholics understand the quoted passage not as forbidding us to make any figures or paintings, or giving any kind of honour to them, but as simply and solely forbidding the making of figures or paintings of any thing *in order to adore them as idols and gods.* They quote, besides, many other passages of the same Bible, in which the figures which God ordered Moses and David to make, and place in the sanctuary in the middle Temple, &c. are mentioned. The same Catholics confirm their interpretation by saying that, if a different explanation be given to the quoted passage, it would imply an open contradiction between the two orders issued by the same Almighty God.

Further, explaining the Greek word " Λατρεια," as meaning the supreme highest religious honour due to God alone, principally by the offering of sacrifices; and stating that in the Catholic Church no sacrifice is offered to Mary the Mother of God, nor to any Angel or Saint, or to any painting or figure of Saints; but only to God alone, and that the Saints are simply honoured as friends and servants of God, and their figures and relics as objects relating to the servants and friends of God; the same Catholics disclaim any participation with idolatry, or with idolatrous superstitions (see St. Augustin "Contra Faustum," lib. v. cap. xix. and lib. xxiv. cap. v.)

§ 15.

On two tenets relating to Lay Magistrates, and to the precept, Not to Kill.

Eneas Sylvius (L. c.) assures us that the Waldenses held, that "A lay magistrate, if wicked and guilty of a mortal sin, does not possess any authority, and that he then is not to be obeyed."[*] And Archbishop Seyssell states, that "They affirmed generally that to kill a man is a mortal sin."[†] Nevertheless, it does not seem that these two tenets can be put in the roll of their unchanged religious opinions. Because they at any rate retracted the former before the middle of the sixteenth century, when they professed "To acknowledge the Princes of the earth." And in relation to the latter, the same Archbishop Seyssell remarks, that "The Waldenses of his time did not hold it unconditionally, but made some exception, for instance, when a man is executed in accordance with the laws of justice, for public vengeance," &c.

---

[*] *Qui mortalis culpæ reus sit, eum neque Sæculari neque Ecclesiastica dignitate pollere, neque parendum ei.* (Eneas Sylvius.)

[†] *Omne homicidium mortale peccatum esse affirmant.* (Seyssell.)

Catholic Doctrine.

Every legitimate magistrate is to be obeyed as far as concerns his lawful authority, as St. Paul says (Rom. xiii. 2), that " He that resisteth the power, resisteth the ordinance of God; and they that resist purchase to themselves damnation." And with St. Peter (1 Eph. ii.) they repeat : " Fear God. Honour the King. Servants be subject to your masters with all fear, not only to the good and gentle, but also to the froward."

In relation to the precept, Not to kill, the Catholics, whilst maintaining that every wilful murder and suicide is a mortal sin; at the same time admit that there are instances in which the destruction of man's life is not to be accounted to be a sin : as when a criminal deserving capital punishment is condemned and put to death; when soldiers are fighting and killing in time of lawful war; and also when it happens that a man occasionally kills another in self-defence, or through some innocent mistake, &c. Therefore, if the Waldenses admitted alike exceptions, there could not have been any disagreement on this point between them and the Catholics.

Section IV.

RELIGIOUS TENETS ADOPTED AT A LATER PERIOD BY THE BOHEMIAN WALDENSES BEFORE THE TIME OF LUTHER AND CALVIN.

AFTER having related the principal tenets of the ancient Waldenses, I will now quote some of the articles contained in that Waldensian confession of faith, which their Bohemian brethren sent to Wladislaus, King of Hungary, in the year 1508 ("Rerum Bohem. Antiqui Scriptores," by Freber. Hanoviæ, 1602). As I undertook to mention the religious doctrines held by the Waldenses before the time of Luther and Calvin, I feel myself obliged to say something on the said confession of faith, on account of its having been written before the time of the said reformers.

In the fourteenth century John Wickliff rose in England, and in the following century John Huss in Bohemia. These two followed the Waldenses in nearly all their tenets enumerated in our last section, and on this ground Wickliff and Huss might be styled Waldensian disciples, though they added many more articles of their own, at variance with the universal Church. Thence it naturally happened that the Bohemian Waldenses, though in some way their masters, in other points followed the novelties of their disciples.

§ 1.

THE TENET OF THE BOHEMIAN WALDENSES ON
AURICULAR CONFESSION.

"The Bohemian Waldenses held that Auricular Confession is useless, and that it is enough to confess our sins to God." (Eneas Sylvius, "Bohem. Hist." [*] [a]

CATHOLIC DOCTRINE.

There is an obligation imposed by our Lord upon Christians to confess their grievous sins to the authorized priests.[a]

---

[*] *Auricularem Confessionem asseverat esse; sufficere enim quemque Deo confiteri peccata.* (Eneas Sylvius, l. c.)

---

[a] The reason generally alleged against Auricular Confession is chiefly this, that God alone knows men's hearts, and He alone forgives the repentant sinners.

[a] The Catholics, on the authority of the Gospels understood in accordance with the old Tradition of the Church, hold that Auricular Confession of sins is commanded to Christians by our Lord with His positive precept, when He said (John xx. 23): "whose sins you shall forgive, they are forgiven them, and whose sins you shall retain, they are retained." And in support of this doctrine, they quote the Acts of the Apostles (xix. 18), St. James (v. 16), Origen (= Hom. 2 in Levit. ad Hom. 2 in Ps. 37), St. Cyprian (= De Lapsis) St. Gregory of Nyssa (= Adversus eos qui conversiones indignant."), St. Basil (in "Reg. Brev." 288), St. Augustin (Hom. 49, ex lib. 50 Hom.), St. Leo the Great (Ep. 91, ad "Theod. Epis."), &c. &c. And in relation to the Decree of the General Council of Lateran, under Innocent III., in the year 1215, obliging every adult Christian to confess his sins to the lawful Priest at least once a year, the Catholics remark that it was not a law establishing Auricular Confession for the first time (as Auricular Confession of sins is a part of the Sacrament of Penance instituted by our Lord), but a simple law of the Church, directing Christians not to allow a year to pass without fulfilling this already existing divine precept of confessing their grievous sins.

§ 2.

Another change in the Waldensian doctrine, and a very substantial one, is the definition of the Church. They say (L. c. p. 240), " That the holy Catholic Church, which they believe is the whole of the elect from the beginning of the world to its end." But that in relation to the ministries, " They believe that the holy Catholic Church is the congregation of all Ministers and people obeying the Divine will, and by obedience united under the same subjection from the beginning till the consummation of all times." Which is in substance the definition printed by Morland in the Catechism, in shape of dialogue, between the Barba and the Infant. " The Church of God" (it is said there) " comprises in her substance the whole of the elect of God; but, in what relates to her ministry, the Church of God comprises the Ministers with the people subject to them, and participating in the same ministries through faith, hope, and charity."

CATHOLIC DEFINITION OF THE CHURCH OF GOD
ON EARTH.

The Catholics, regarding the quoted definitions as confused as well as very gratuitous in what relates to the Church of God on this earth, which ought to be *Visible, One, Holy, Catholic*, or *Universal and Apostolic;* reject them, and thus define the Church of God on earth:

"The Church is the society of all those who profess the faith and the doctrine of Christ; which Church Christ, the Prince of Shepherds, confided to the Apostle Peter and his Successors * to be ruled and governed." *

---

* *Ecclesia est omnium Christi fidem atque doctrinam profitentium universitas, quam princeps pastorum Christus tum Petro Apostolo tum hujus Successoribus gubernandam tradidit atque gubernandam.* (Peter Canisius, "Christian Doctrine," Colonia, 1577, p. 131).

---

* The writer of this definition of the Church illustrates and explains its last part with many authorities; and concludes with that well known passage of one of the oldest fathers of the Church, quoted and praised also by Tertullian, St. Irenæus ("Adversus Hæres." lib. iii. cap. iii.), who says that "It is necessary that all Churches, namely, all believers existing in every part of the world, should unite to the Church of Rome for the sake of her powerful primacy, and for her having kept the Tradition of the Apostles:" *Ad hanc Ecclesiam propter potentiorem* (ubi potiorem) *principalitatem necesse est omnem convenire Ecclesiam, hoc est, eos qui sunt undique fideles; in qua semper ab his qui sunt undique conservata est ea quæ est ab Apostolic Traditio."*

§ 3.

THE TENET OF THE BOHEMIAN WALDENSES ON THE HOLY COMMUNION.

"It is necessary to receive the Holy Eucharist under the two kinds of bread and wine." ("Rerum. Bohem. Script." L. c. p. 250).[*]

CATHOLIC DOCTRINE.

It is not commanded, nor necessary, that laymen should receive the Holy Communion under the two kinds of bread and wine.[**]

---

[*] The Bohemian Waldenses supported their assertion by that passage of the Gospel in which it is said, that without eating the flesh and drinking the blood of the Lord, we shall not have life in us.

[**] While admitting that at the beginning of Christianity, laymen received generally the communion under the two kinds of bread and wine, when they assisted at the celebration of the Holy mysteries; the Catholics, in support of their doctrine, make the following remarks:—1st, That even in the Primitive Church, the Holy Communion, when not administered to those present at the time of the celebration of the Holy mysteries, was given under the kind of bread alone, not only to the laity, but also to the Priests and Bishops. 2nd, That as our Saviour assumed our human nature, soul and body, in unity of His Divine Person, and as His living body is undivided from His Divine blood; to receive the communion under one kind (any of

bread) alone is to receive at the same time His blood. 3rd, That, in consequence, an equal grace is given to those who receive our Lord under the two kinds, or under the kind of bread alone, if they are equally well disposed in their souls. 4th, That to give the communion under the two kinds, or under the kind of bread alone, is a matter left to the discretion of the Church, as is the case with all other practices which do not pertain to the substance of Sacraments (see the "Council of Trent," sess. 21, ch. i., and sqq.). For these reasons, the Catholics conclude that it is not necessary to receive the Holy Eucharist under the two kinds of bread and wine; and that the Church had and has the lawful power to prescribe to the laity, and to the Priests and Bishops, when they are not themselves celebrating the Holy Mysteries, to receive the communion under the kind of bread alone.

§ 4.

THE TENET OF THE BOHEMIAN WALDENSES ON TRANSUBSTANTIATION.

"The Bohemian Waldenses rejected admittance to the word 'Transubstantiation' in reference to the Mystery of Euchariay." ("Rerum Bohem. Script." L. C. p. 264).[a]

CATHOLIC STATEMENT ON THE SAME.

The doctrine expressed by the word "Transubstantiation" is founded on the written and the traditional Word of God, and has been always believed in the Church.[b]

---

[a] The word *Transubstantiation*, adopted by that General Council of Lateran, under Innocent III.,—by which the Waldenses were condemned in 1215—was rejected by the Bohemian Waldenses, after having adopted with Wickliff the tenet that the substance of bread and wine remains in the Eucharist after the words of consecration, as the Lutherans also did afterwards. Yet the same Bohemian Waldenses, in this confession of faith, still admit in some degree the real presence of the body of Christ in the Eucharist, as appears from the following words (L. c. pag. 261): "*Dicimus entem et simpliciter confitemur quod inibi est vere Deus et verus Dominus Jesus Christus, et quod est in Sacramento cum sua naturali corpore tubis sed per aliam citarationem quam in dextris Dei, et adhuc dicimus quod est etiam cum verus spiritali.*"

[b] The doctrine of the Catholic Church expressed by the word *Transubstantiation*, is this, that when a duly consecrated Priest pronounces officially the words of consecration on the bread and wine, then, by the power of the Almighty, the substance of the bread and of the wine is changed into the substance of the body and blood of Christ, notwithstanding the outline, and form, and taste of bread and wine remaining unchanged. And this doctrine is derived both from the Evangelists, and from the sayings of St. Paul (ad Cor. Ep. 1), and is explained by the old Fathers of the Church. I will quote here, as an instance, the expressions of St. Cyril of Jerusalem ("Cat. 4 Mystag."): "When Christ himself then affirms and says of the bread, 'This is my body,' who is there afterwards who should dare to be doubtful? Once he changed the water into wine by his holy will, and is it not right to believe him, that he had changed the wine into blood? Therefore, let us receive the body and blood of Christ with all certainty. Because, under the species of bread, is given his body to you, and under the species of wine, is given to you his blood. Keep it as most certain that the bread which we see is not bread, though to any taste is seems bread, but it is the body of Christ; and the wine which we see, though to the taste appears to be wine, it is not wine, but it is the blood of Christ." *Quare cum omni certitudine corpus et sanguinem Christi sumamus. Nam sub specie panis datur tibi corpus, et sub specie vini datur sanguis . . . Pro certissimo habeas panem hunc qui videtur a nobis non esse panem, etiamsi gustus panem esse sentiat, sed esse corpus Christi, et vinum quod a nobis recipieritis, tametsi sensui gustus vinum esse videatur, non tamen vinum, sed sanguinem esse Christi.*

K

CONCLUSION.

IT has been clearly proved, by means of undeniable authorities, that the Waldenses had their first origin in the second half of the twelfth century, and that Peter of Vaud, the rich merchant of Lyons, was their founder; that the persecutions endured by the Waldenses in Piemont were chiefly caused by their transgressing the laws of the country and the orders of their civil rulers; that the barbarities described by an unfaithful historian, and on his authority published by other writers, as perpetrated against them in the year 1655, are all mere inventions of a deceiver; and that the religious opinions adopted by the same Waldenses, after separating from the Universal Church, are not the doctrines taught by our Lord or his Apostles.

The gentle reader, who has seen and perused this little volume, not commendable indeed for its elocution and style, but yet entitled to some consideration on account of the authorities and documents herein contained, will, I hope, take now the trouble to cast his eyes again on my preface, and compare the established historical facts with the unwarranted assertions related there to have been made at a meeting held last year at the London residence of a noble Duke. In making this comparison, he will be surprised at seeing the old saying confirmed, that "There is nothing so clear and certain that may not be easily distorted by false assertions and sophistries." In fact, none of those bold assertions there made, can stand when brought face to face with the real facts. Every proposition stated there is not only incorrect, but has not any foundation of truth. It is not true that the "Waldenses had guarded the primitive Christianity of the Apostles for at least six-

teen hundred years." They appeared the first time only
six hundred years ago. It is not true, that " The beginning
of their belief is unknown." By a great number of contemporaries it is proved that they separated from the
Universal Church, of whom they were children, in the second
half of the twelfth century. And, setting aside the other
assertions respecting their doctrines and sufferings, so fully
contradicted in the second and third parts, it is not true
that Irenæus, the glorious Bishop and Martyr of Lyons,
" Had founded in the second century a Church for the Waldenses." They did not exist until ten centuries after his
time. That St. Irenæus, the champion of the Apostolical
succession of the Roman Pontiffs, the assertor of the Traditions of the Church, the conqueror of all heresies, can be
stated to have founded a Church for those who resisted the
Roman Church, rejected the Traditions of the ancient
Fathers, and held doctrines characterized as heretical by
the same Church, is most intolerable and calumnious.

The labour I have undergone in collecting and putting
in order and commenting upon the documents published,
many of them for the first time, in this volume, will not be
despised, I hope, by those learned men who, being free from
prejudiced opinions, will be glad to see some better light
shining upon the Waldensian origin and facts. These facts
have too often been distorted and misrepresented, on account of the narrative of John Leger being taken as a true
historical statement. It will be a full reward to me, and
will cause me to forget the tediousness of my labour, if
these persons will judge that I have not lost my time,
and am giving to the public a volume not altogether un-
profitable.

Before ending I cannot disguise my fear in relation to
another class of persons, who have the idea deeply rooted
in their mind that the Waldenses are the link of the golden
chain connecting the Protestants and new Reformers with
the Apostles and disciples of the Primitive Church. When

hearing of a book which shows clearly that the imaginary link does not exist, and that the Apostolical origin, the innocent conduct, and the pure doctrine of the old Waldenses cannot be maintained; they will, perhaps, rise up against my little work. I can well imagine that some of this class will at least say that this publication is only good for mischief; that it is contrary to the persuasion of all the good friends of the Vaudois; and that it would have been much better to have left matters as they stood for centuries. Such persons may be compared to that man mentioned by Horace, who, instead of being grateful to his friends for having restored him to his senses, reproached them in these words: "By Jove! you have killed and not saved me, friends, by taking thus forcibly away my pleasure and the most pleasing rambling of my mind." *

I conclude by saying to those, who are more influenced by party spirit than by a love of truth, that no objection against this poor volume will be conclusive, if the Documents brought forward here are not proved to be false.

---

* *Pol! me occidistis, amici,*
Non servastis, ait; cui sic extorta voluptas,
Et demptus per vim mentis gratissimus error.
(Hor. Epistol. lib. ii. ep. ii. ad Julium Florum.)

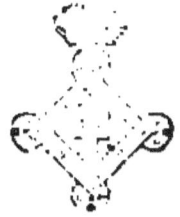

INDEX.

CHISWICK PRESS: PRINTED BY WHITTINGHAM AND WILKINS, TOOKS COURT, CHANCERY LANE.

CORRIGENDA.

Page 23, line 17, *for* " taught " *read* " thought."

Page 73, line 19, *for* " Sir James Morland " *read* " Sir Samuel Morland."

Page 68, line 24, *read* " the extract of his narrative as nearly as possible in his own words."

Page 99, line 17, *for* " pense " *read* " pause."

Page 131, line 2, *for* " six " *read* " seven."

Page 133, 1st col. l. 26, p. 134, 2nd col. l. 20, *for* " Alexander " *read* " Innocent."